Daniel Publishing
2021

The Ultimate Science-Fiction ANTHOLOGY

COLLECTION OF SHORT STORIES FROM THE 50's

Book #1 : Terror Station

Front cover painting by H. W. McCauley, illustrating "Terror Station" Interior illustrations by W. F. Terry, and Lloyd Rognan; cartoons by Stan Fine, George Ludway, Luther Scheffy, and Bill Reid.

If you have any question, contact us at danielpublishings@gmx.fr
If you like this book, feel free to let us a comment on our Amazon product page !
This is a restoration of an old material. The quality of the print can sometime reflects
the age of the documents.

Originally published by

Introducing the AUTHOR

★

Dwight V. Swain

★

AUTOBIOGRAPHY, Br'er Hamling says—and me with a deadline to meet. In fact, half-a-dozen deadlines.

But here goes:

Full name, Dwight Vreeland Swain. Born Nov. 17, 1915, at Rochester, Mich. Grew up mostly at Jackson, Mich. B. A. and Certificate in Journalism, University of Michigan, 1937. Married (to Margaret Simpson, professional voice and accompanist) at Chicago Aug. 6, 1942. Served (publications and information-education) in the AUS from Oct. 6, 1942, to Jan. 25, 1946. One son, Thomas McCray Swain, born July 16, 1946. M. A., University of Oklahoma, 1954.

Jobs? I've worked as a newspaperman in Michigan, Pennsylvania, New York, Illinois, California, Oklahoma . . . peddled gadgets door-to-door and as a pitchman . . . followed the crops . . . shipped as an ordinary seaman . . dealt blackjack in Philadelphia . . . hustled packingcases in San Francisco . . . press-agented for a mind-reader . . . interviewed murderers for the true crime books . . . helped edit *Flying* without ever having been up in an airplane. . .

But writing has always held my private spotlight. I first sold nonfiction (to a Sunday-school paper) before I finished high school; fiction, to *Fantastic Adventures* in 1941. My pulp fiction sales (stf, western, detective, adventure) passed the million-word mark a long

(*Concluded on Page* 131)

INTRODUCING the Author

★ Dwight V. Swain ★

(Concluded from Page 2)

while back; and at one time I even spent four years as a full-time free-lance.

I've always doted on sci-fic, both as reader and writer. Took my first whack at it for *Wonder Stories* as a kid—and promptly got a rejection that informed me that my science was "illogical and incorrect."

Fair enough. It probably was. I'm afraid science always takes a beating when it gets in the way of my wilder extrapolations. To me, the story's the thing.

I'll even rationalize my position. For over and over again, in working with technical experts, I've found that they're the first to tell you that what's absolute truth today may turn out to be completely haywire tomorrow. And as for day after tomorrow—well, most of them won't even hazard a guess.

Like most writers, I'd infinitely rather talk than write. But I've also learned—the hard way—that talking doesn't give you anywhere near the sense of achievement that you get when you see your stuff in print or on the screen. An unproductive week makes me uneasy. Stretch it to be a month and I'm miserable with frustration.

Which brings me to my setup since 1952.

It's one that strikes me as darn' close to ideal. Half the time I teach writing at the University of Oklahoma; the other half I free-lance.

The teaching (which I handle largely through individual manuscript criticism conferences) balances the loneliness of writing. It also gives me some interesting sidelights on practical psychology, plus the satisfaction of seeing students chalk up first sales to markets from the Saturday Evening Post and Houghton-Mifflin on down.

My free-lancing, on the other hand, both bolsters my income and buoys my ego. Mostly, these days, I concentrate on scripts for educational and promotional films. But every once in a while the yen to whack out fiction grows too strong and I come up with such a yarn as TERROR STATION.

Hope you like it.

—Dwight V. Swain

The Editorial.....

AN *ACTION story is more popular than any other type.* That's a positive statement if we ever heard—or made one! The funny thing is, it's true! At least, that's been our experience in the editorial profession from way back in the days when we edited *Amazing Stories & Fantastic Adventures*, down to the present in our editing of *Imagination*, companion magazine to *Tales*.

ALL of which leads up to a very important decision we had to make in the past few weeks. As you know, we've been following a program of humorous-type fiction in *Tales*. Sadly enough—and we're not ashamed to admit it—sales figures were not encouraging enough to continue that policy. So, bowing to your wishes as readers, we make an abrupt about-face editorially. Action stories—the kind you can't put down until you're finished reading the entire piece—are the order of the day.

YOU'LL note which author we selected to inaugurate this policy: Dwight V. Swain. Many of you who are readers of *Imagination* will be familiar with Dwight's work—as will those of you old-time science fiction fans who used to read his great stories in *Amazing Stories* in the early and middle forties. Dwight Swain writes an action story in the tradition of Edgar Rice Burroughs—

which is to say, plenty of adventure, with fast pace and a good science fiction background. What's even more important, he writes a darned fine *entertaining* story! So turn to page 6 and have yourself a good time!

YOU'LL note the new-type covers too. Like them better? We've got some humdingers coming up with even more action! All in all, you won't find *IMAGINATIVE TALES* dull in any way—we promise you! See you next issue . . .wlh

"Yes, sir, crazy as it sounds, he swears he saw a flying pencil!"

4

Terror Station

by

Dwight V. Swain

It was sheer madness — monstrous creatures appearing out of nowhere at a top-secret desert Base. Yet Stone knew it was not madness he was fighting but a vicious enemy.   The Stake: Earth!

7

HE saw the woman first. Blindly, she stumbled out of the moonless desert night a hundred yards ahead, into the dim right edge of the path slashed by his headlights. Lurching, staggering, she scuffed through the gravel of the highway's shoulder; reached the asphalt and took two short, uncertain steps out on it, swaying as if the sudden change to smoother footing had almost made her lose her balance.

Stone jammed on his brakes.

Only then, before the car could even start to stop, movement flickered in the murk from which the woman had emerged. Stone glimpsed a shifting scarlet glow, a dipping, twisting streak of color. Oozing through the backdrop of the night, it drew swiftly closer to the roadway and the woman . . . then faded, swallowed up in the glare of the approaching headlights.

But as it vanished, a spot of strange translucence materialized to replace it.

Formless, almost without perceptible substance, the splotch moved faster now, gliding across the shoulder and out onto the highway.

Beyond it, the woman half-turned; threw a frantic glance back along the way from which she'd come even as she took another stumbling step.

In the same instant, the translucence swept down upon her.

The woman's face contorted. Sheer terror etched her features, so deep that even Stone could see it. She tried to lunge away.

But now gleaming tendrils lanced forth from the translucence, curled about her, held her helpless.

The woman screamed.

That scream: It echoed even through the shriek of Stone's scorching tires, seared itself into his brain so deep that he never would, never could, forget it.

Then, abruptly, the scream cut off. The translucence swirled back towards the roadside and the shadows, dragging the woman with it.

Savagely, Stone jerked the steering wheel right with all his might, trying to follow the horror with his headlights. Skidding, the car rocked round on two wheels. For a spine-chilling split second Stone thought it was going to go over. But at the last moment it righted itself and shuddered to a halt in a choking cloud of dust beyond the shoulder.

Straight ahead, woman and translucence hung spotlighted less than fifty feet away.

Stone snatched his Colt from its holster on the steering post. Leaping from the car, he raced forward.

It was as if the sight of him gave the woman new strength. Her whole body convulsed. Tearing free from the monstrous thing that held her, she lurched towards Stone, blood streaming from a dozen wounds.

The translucence seemed to swell and darken. Then, in a rush, it hurtled towards the woman.

But now Stone was abreast of her. Cat-footed, he leaped between her and the monster; he blazed three fast shots into its center.

The shining surface quivered. For the fraction of a second it drew back.

Stone could see the creature more clearly now. Murkily transparent as oily water, it stood nearly a head taller than his own six feet.

Except that it didn't have any head.

Instead, a barrel body splayed out into many thin, cable-like tentacles at top and bottom, each terminating in a round disc the size of a quarter. Its only truly opaque matter appeared to be concentrated in a narrow, dully scarlet band perhaps three inches wide that girded the center of its body.

Staring at it, Stone wondered if he were somehow going mad.

Then, abruptly, there was no more time for thinking, observation. With a rush, lunged towards him, lower tentacles as if they many skillfully-coordinated feet.

Behind Stone, the woman cried out: "The light—! Watch out for the light!"

STONE glimpsed it as she spoke: A small, lensed cube of box that suddenly shot out at the end of one of the creature's upper tentacles.

He leaped sidewise.

Almost in the same instant, a vivid purple streak blazed from the box.

It missed Stone by inches. Desperately, he snapped a wild shot at the lens, then fired twice more in the onrushing monster's midriff.

This time, the thing didn't even hesitate.

Stone jerked the trigger again.

A hollow click. The gun was empty.

With a curse, Stone hurled it at the nightmare thing before him. Then, whirling, he raced headlong back towards his car.

Like an evil, gleaming shadow, the monster sped after him. It moved fast—horribly, incredibly fast.

Panting, Stone veered left, not even daring to look back. The headlights blazed blindingly into his eyes.

Something brushed his shoulder. He felt his shirt rip.

Then he was past the lights. Twisting, he dived headlong beneath the car, heedless of the gravel that slashed his face and chest and knees and shins and belly. Driving his elbows into the dirt, he whipped himself out on the far side of the vehicle.

A tentacle groped for his heel.

Savagely, he stamped the disc against a rock.

The tentacle jerked back. Sobbing for breath, Stone scrambled to his knees and clutched the door-handle.

He got the door open just as another tentacle came through the window on the far side of the car, reaching for him.

Cursing, he jerked back barely in time, slammed the door shut on the tentacle with all his strength.

The latch caught. The car shook as the monster tried to writhe away.

Stone spun about. In three steps he was at the trunk—clawing aside his luggage, breaking his nails on the jack.

His hand closed around the axe-handle in the same instant that the car gave a sudden lurch. There was a sound like that of a gigantic rubber band snapping. Then, like an echo, a tentacle-disc slapped against his right ribs just below the armpit.

Clutching the axe, Stone leaped back.

But the disc clung as if it were part of him. Agony exploded around it, tearing at his flesh. Before he could shake the red haze of pain from his eyes, the monster—free of the car now—was upon him.

Convulsively, Stone swung the axe.

It bounced off the barrel body as if it had struck solid rubber. More discs slapped at him.

Stone staggered, axe sagging. The tentacles had him now—constricting, engulfing. He lurched against the monster; felt the discs' pressure growing, seeking to rend his very body.

Pain-knotted, barely conscious, he twisted the axe-blade against the opaque scarlet band that girded the creature's midriff.

Reflex-like, a disc low on his spine jerked him back, away.

Stone forgot the agony, the pain-haze. Fiercely, he slashed out with the axe.

A surge of triumph raced through him as its blade bit deep into the unshielded scarlet band.

Now the tentacles tore at him in frenzy, clutched at the axe.

Before they could seize it, Stone swung again—horizontally, this time, so that the rubbery body might have no chance to deflect the cutting edge from the nerve-band.

The blade struck home with a sound like that of a melon shattering on pavement. Clear to the eye it sank—

The tentacles hurled Stone backward, slamming him hard against the side of his car as they let go their hold. He sagged there, raw-nerved and sick and bleeding.

Shambling, uncertain, the monster moved away . . . away—and towards the spot where the woman still lay prone and silent.

With an effort, Stone dragged himself erect. Then, axe still in hand, he stumbled after the nightmare creature.

The thing speeded its pace.

Stone forced himself to a run, cutting wide around his adversary.

Ten seconds later, he stood between it and the woman.

The creature hesitated.

STONE bared his teeth in a savage grimace. The fact that he had outdistanced the hideous thing; that it paused now, grasping and indecisive—such were more than enough to strip away his own pain and weariness.

"Damn you!" he grated harshly. "We'll see who gets her!"

He lifted the axe; took a quick step forward.

The monster fell back before him.

Then, of a sudden, a tentacle speared out.

—The tentacle with the light-box.

Stone charged in, swinging, as the purple streak blazed forth.

The creature shifted, undulating away from the axe. The streak of purple fire missed Stone.

Missed, by far too wide a margin to be coincidence.

Like an echo, a choked cry of agony rose behind him.

Stone spun about, numb panic flaring in him.

The woman no longer lay limp and prostrate. Now, instead, her whole body jerked in a continuing spasm. Her hands clutched her side, and her lips spilled blood.

Stone whirled again, back to the monster.

But the creature was already fleeing—gliding out of the arc of the headlights' beam, into the empty blackness of the desert. Even as Stone glimpsed it, the night swallowed it up.

Only a lunatic would have followed.

With a snarl of frustration, Stone ran to the woman; dropped on his knees beside her.

Her whole side was burned black where the purple beam had struck. She clutched his hand, her nails biting deep. "Kill me, quick!

Please! I can't stand it—"

Sweat stood out on Stone's forehead. Desperately, he forced his voice gentle, level: "Easy, now. You'll be all right. I'll get you to my car. It's only a couple of miles to the proving ground—"

"No, no. I can't stand it. I'm dying—" The woman's voice trailed off in a bubbling scream. Her body twisted. Then: "Maybe —my husband—the robots—back there beyond the mesa—"

"Easy . . ." Stone whispered. But his lips were dry.

"My . . . my husband . . ."

A shudder ran through the woman's body. Then, suddenly, she sagged limp.

Dead.

Sickness twisted at Stone's belly. Gently, he crossed the woman's arms across her breasts . . . straightened the tormented twisted body . . . wiped away the blood and smoothed the dark hair back from the small, plain face.

She was young, he saw now; far younger than he'd thought—not more than twenty-five at most.

So young . . . and so dead.

And somewhere, out there in the desert night, lurked the creature that had killed her.

And what was it the dying woman had said, about robots on a mesa—?

Stone's spine prickled. Stiffly,

he started to get up.

Only then, out of the night, a voice clipped, "Hold it!"

A chill, somehow familiar voice.

Stone froze.

"That's it. And get your hands out where we can see 'em."

Wordless, Stone obeyed.

"Now turn so the light shines on your face."

Again, obedience.

"Well! If it isn't our Mister Stone!" The words carried an ugly inflection. And then: "Come on, you guys . . ."

Figures converged from the blackness—erect, helmeted, uniformed figures, armed with rifles and carbines.

Soldiers.

The tension drained out of Stone. Of a sudden he felt weak, wobbly, half-hysterical.

And that voice—of course it was familiar!

"Sergeant Bjornberg," he announced, "I've never been so glad to see anybody in my life!"

He dropped his hands.

Instantly, a gun-barrel gouged his back. "Keep those hands out!"

"What—?" Stone stared. "Sergeant, you know me . . ."

"Do I? Don't try to pull any fast ones on me, mister!" The sergeant moved into view as he spoke. His usually good-humored features showed heavy now, set in sullen lines. Striding over to the woman, he flashed a light onto her dead face. "Well, now! Ain't this pretty!"

With an effort, Stone held his temper. "The way she was killed was anything but pretty, sergeant. And the thing that did the job is still running loose. I'd suggest you post a heavy guard, then get me to headquarters as soon as possible."

The sergeant sneered openly. "*You're* telling *me* what to do?"

"I'm merely suggesting." In spite of himself, Stone's voice took on a brittle edge. "However, I do happen to have charge of certain aspects of security for this area, and I doubt that Captain Hayes would think I was out of line."

"Oh?" Sergeant Bjornberg grinned—an ugly grin, utterly without mirth. "Well, I think I got a better idea, *Mister* Stone."

"Well?"

"I'll post a guard, all right; and I'll take you to headquarters."

"Fair enough."

"But I'll do it my own way, you lousy civilian phony—and that's under arrest, as a prisoner and a murder suspect!"

CHAPTER II

GLINES' taste ran to richly aromatic tobaccos. Even now, long after midnight, his office hung heavy with the stink of the stuff.

Stone wrinkled his nose in distaste, again shifted his weight in the hard chair, trying to ease his aching muscles. The welts where the monster's discs had clutched him stung like new burns. Bruises and scratches plagued him every time he moved, a continuing, continuous irritation.

And still Glines did not come.

Now, in the silence, the ticking of the leather-embellished desk clock seemed to grow louder, till the sound of it echoed in Stone's ears like an infuriating off-key drumbeat. He found himself resenting the desk itself, with its precise, too-neat arrangement of office trivia. The air the lazy ceiling fan pushed against his face pressed thick as warm, wet cheesecloth.

Yet his mouth stayed dry. When a rill of icy sweat trickled from his armpit, it sent a tremor through his whole body.

He gritted his teeth, squeezed his eyes tight shut, trying to shut out the awful memory of the monster and the woman.

But shutting his eyes only made the picture come back clearer, sharper. Better to leave them open . . .

Once more, he shifted cursing under his breath as new pain pulsed through him.

Besides, the chair creaked.

Stone frowned. It was idiotic, the way he found himself giving way to every tiny irritation . . . almost as if the whole base—this office especially—somehow had come to radiate tension.

And tension was one thing he couldn't afford just now.

Grimly, he sucked in air—a deep breath that filled his lungs . . . held it for the count of ten . . . expelled it in a rush, letting himself go limp and jelly-like.

The third time he did it, he knew that some of the raw-nerved stiffness was leaving him. Closing his eyes no longer conjured up macabre visions.

Now, however, he found his mind turning to Bjornberg.

The sergeant's open hostility baffled him. In the past, they'd always been on a pleasant enough footing—friends, almost. Back in his service days, he'd even soldiered in some of the same places as had the sergeant. It gave them a common ground of past and interest, something to talk about over a beer.

Yet tonight, Bjornberg had called him a "lousy civilian' phony".

Stone shook his head slowly. It just didn't make sense.

He became aware that the clock's tick was growing louder again . . . fraying at his nerves—

Then, abruptly, footsteps echoed in the hall outside. The door opened. Glines waddled in.

It was typical that he should be freshly shaven and fully dressed, even to tie and clean white shirt. Emergencies might come and go; but if they wanted Glines' attention, they'd have to wait till the last button was properly secured and the pink chops smooth and anointed with perfumed shaving lotion.

With an effort, Stone kept his voice pleasant. "Hi, Herb. Sorry to drag you out with this nonsense."

"Nonsense—?" Glines' fat face stayed stiff, his manner unbending. "I'm not sure I like your choice of words there, Stone."

Stone stared "Herb! What is this? Just because you take over my job for two weeks while they call me in to Washington—"

"Don't evade the issue, Stone!" Glines posed, too erect, beside the desk. His lips pursed. "As I see it, neither your job nor your trip to Washington has anything to do with the things Sergeant Bjornberg's told me."

"I see." Stone clipped his words. "In that case, Glines, maybe we'd better get a few things straight. It happens I'm your superior here. And if I'm not 'Carl' to you, then I'm damn' well 'Mister Stone.' Is that clear?"

"No."

"What—?"

"No, I said. It isn't clear—not clear at all." Glines stood openly defiant, insulting. Insolently, he thrust out his puffy lower lip. "You talk a lot about being my superior here, don't you? Well, as of this moment, I'm not at all sure that you are."

Stone drew a deep, incredulous breath. Then, slowly—very slowly—he came up from his chair. When he spoke, his words were measured: "Glines, you're either drunk or crazy. In either case, I'm sick of it. The MP's have my statement of the facts of what happened tonight. I'm worn out, and I went to get a shower and have the medics disinfect these cuts and then go to bed. This cross-examination business can wait till morning."

He turned on his heel, strode towards the door.

Behind him, a drawer rattled. Glines' voice rang, shrill and angry:

"Oh, no, you don't!"

Stone ignored him.

"Stone! Stop or I'll shoot!"

Stone came up short; half-turned, staring.

GLINES stood crouched behind the desk, his eyes black, beady slits above fat cheeks. He gripped an automatic, a heavy Army Colt, in one pudgy hand.

"Back!" he cried shrilly. "Come back here, Stone, before I shoot you like you deserve!"

Stone stood very still, trying without avail to fathom the things that seethed in the black eyes.

First Bjornberg; now Glines. Had the whole base gone mad?

"Easy, Herb," he said soothingly. "Easy does it. I'll come back."

Careful of every movement, he made his way to the desk. "You can put the gun down now, Herb. I won't try to leave again till you say to."

"I'll say you won't!" Glines bared uneven teeth in a taunting smile. And then: "Oh, you were clever, all right, Stone. But not clever enough to fool me."

"I wasn't?"

"No. It all came to me in a flash as soon as Bjornberg told me about you and that woman, and the crazy story you tried to put out about fighting some monster."

Glines' face grew more flushed as he spoke, his words and breathing jerky and uneven. The hand that held the gun quivered.

New prickles of tension touched Stone's spine. "Sure, Herb; sure . . ."

It was as if his fat little aide hadn't even heard him; as if the man were talking to himself, almost.

"The minute I woke up, it all clicked into place. Just like that." Glines giggled, high and ragged. "Oh, I'd been suspicious all along, of course. I checked your record while you were gone—the way you sneaked into security work, pretending to be an American agent while you fought with the Communists in Spain; the business of playing professional soldier in China; those years you spent with the OSS during the war. You cut quite a figure, all right. It made you look tough, dangerous, trustworthy, experienced. But it was all aimed at just one thing: This job here, in charge of civilian security on the country's top top-secret project. You were willing to wait, to bide your time. Because you knew that when you got this spot here you could really do the job right when you betrayed us!"

A numbness crept over Stone. It was incredible, this mad net of distortion Glines was weaving about him.

Something was behind it, surely . . . some dark and evil pattern.

Yet what—?

It was a question pregnant with frustration. Because he didn't dare to argue; not with an obvious madman. He couldn't even probe too deeply.

He tried to speak calmly: "Did you figure out the rest of it, too, Herb?"

"The rest—?"

"Sure. How it all fits together. How the business about the woman and the monster could help me betray anything?"

Scorn distended Glines' eyes. He radiated contempt. "Do you think I'm completely stupid? I knew it the instant I woke up, of course, just like the rest. You wanted some kind of cover to hide behind so that no one would suspect you when news about the project got out. So you killed that poor woman, then made up the story about the monster. You knew that as soon as it got to the papers there'd be dozen of reporters swarming over the base; you can't guard every inch of a government reservation as big as this one. Then you could blame the reporters for the leak on the project."

"I see." Stone nodded slowly. "Well, I guess you've got it all, then. You might as well call in MacDougal."

"Don't worry. I'll call him." Again Glines giggled. "Only first I'm going to wrap this all up good and tight. You're too good a friend of his for me to take any chances. Besides,"—his eyes grew suddenly cold and wary—"besides, I'm not too sure where he stands. Even a base director's suspect, when he's friends with a traitor!"

STONE made an elaborate business of shrugging. "That's carrying it a little far, isn't it, Herb? Mac's going to have the final report to make on this business, and he might not like it if he thought you were trying to pull a fast one on him."

"If he knew, he might." Glines' eyes glittered. "But then, I plan to handle it more simply than that, without any red tape. Bjornberg understands. He'll take care of it."

"He'll—take care of it?"

"Yes." Glines smirked. "*Ley del fuego,* they call it in Spanish. The law of flight. Shot while attempting to escape."

Stone's palms were suddenly slick with sweat. The ticking of the desk clock echoed in his ears like the knell of doom. He made it a point to breathe deeply, evenly. "That's a big responsibility for a man to take, Herb."

"Let me worry about that, Stone. I think I'll find it a pleasure."

As he spoke, Glines came round the desk, waddling as always.

Ordinarily, the way Glines moved made Stone want to smile. Only now, of a sudden, it wasn't funny.

Especially when the gun the fat man held stayed so very steady.

Abruptly, ignoring the weapons, Stone turned to the desk . . . picked up the clock . . . stared down at its face. "You'd better hurry, then, Herb."

"What—?"

"Time's running out. The sergeant goes off duty in a couple of minutes."

He lifted the clock so Glines could see it.

The black, beady eyes flicked to the dial.

Stone hurled the clock, square at Glines' head.

His aide jerked away, barely in time to dodge the missile.

But in that split second of distraction, reflex movement, Stone lunged in—knocking Glines' gun aside with a left-foreman block, driving a hard right into the pit of the fat man's bulging paunch.

Glines crashed back against the wall, tottered, and slid to the floor his face scarlet as he fought agonizedly for breath.

Stone stomped down on his wrist; kicked the Colt aside. Then, scooping it up, he stood straining his ears, listening for some outside reaction to the scuffle.

None came.

Wordless, he strode to the door.

Panting, now, Glines glared up at him eyes sparking hate. "Go—go ahead—Stone! See—how far—you get!"

"Bjornberg?"

"That's right. I gave him orders to stand guard outside the

building—and to shoot on sight!" Stone smiled thinly. "That's why I'm not going out." He threw the door's heavy bolt in place. "You see, there's just one catch to all your theories, Glines: They're not true. So we're going to get Mac-Dougal down here right now and square things away."

As he spoke, he strode swiftly to the desk; picked up the phone, dialed the base director's quarters number.

Four rings. Then MacDougal's sleep-thickened voice: "Base director speaking."

"Carl Stone, Mac. Get down to Glines' office fast; this is urgent. And it might be smart to bring along a couple of guards."

The sleepiness faded from Mac-Dougal's voice. "Of course, Carl. If you say so." A pause. "I didn't know you were back. When did you get in?"

"Awhile ago. But something's happened I don't want to talk about on the phone, and I can't leave the office, here."

"I'll be there in five minutes."

HE made it in four—a big, shaggy man with shoulders like mine beams and John L. Lewis eyebrows. Two armed guards followed him in.

"You've got troubles, Carl?"

"You might say so. Glines, here'"

—Stone gestured to the fat man, still sitting slumped against the wall —"has suddenly decided I'm a trator. His solution to the problem was to arrange to have me shot while attempting to escape."

MacDougal's shaggy eyebrows lifted. "Well, now! That's one way of eliminating a problem, isn't it? —Though I doubt that he's actually got it in him to pull the trigger when the cards are down."

Stone shrugged. "He didn't plan to."

"No?" The base director cocked his head. "Then who—?"

"Sergeant Bjornberg. Whether he shares Glines' delusions or not, I can't say. But Glines tells me he stationed the sergeant outside the building, with orders to shoot me on sight."

MacDougal frowned. "Things really have been happening to you, haven't they, Carl?" And then, turning to Glines: "How about this, Herb? Got anything to get off your chest?"

The fat man scrambled to his feet and stood pompously erect in a belated effort to regain his dignity. His eyes sparked. "I certainly do, Mr. MacDougal. There's not a word of truth in what he says—about the shooting part, that is. What actually happened was, Sergeant Bjornberg caught him down the road a couple of miles, crouched over a woman's corpse. You can see how cut up he is"—a contemptuous gesture towards Stone—"as if they'd fought before he killed her. He tried to alibi himself with a wild story about them both being attacked by some bug-eyed monster—"

MacDougal interrupted: "You can skip that part, Glines. The driver from the motor pool told me about it on the way over."

"Yes, sir." Glines nodded tightly. "Well, anyhow, after he'd given his story to the MP's, Sergeant Bjornberg still wasn't satisfied. Under the circumstances, and all, and what with Stone acting so peculiar, he asked me to come over and talk to him. When I got here, Stone was ugly and insulting. He refused to talk to me, and insisted on going to his quarters. I was already worried about the way he was acting, so when he got so hostile I pulled a gun on him. After all"—he flushed—"we were alone here. I hadn't thought to have a guard stand by."

"And then—?"

"He attacked me. I didn't want to shoot him, of course, and he's stronger than I am. He got hold of the gun, and then called you."

MacDougal frowned; studied the floor briefly. Then, after a moment, he turned to Stone: "Well, Carl?"

Stone could feel heat rising in his face. "What do you mean, 'Well, Carl'? Glines picked a fight with me from the moment he walked into this room. He accused me of being a traitor, went through a long rigamarole about how I was to leak informaton on the project—"

"If you'll check his record, you'll see that I have ample reason for thinking as I do, Mr. MacDougal!" Glines broke in sharply. "He fought with the Communists in Spain. He trained troops at Yenan. He went into Yugoslavia for the OSS; served more than a year with the Partisans. He's a Communist and a traitor, I tell you—"

Of a sudden, Stone's patience ran out. Inside him, something snapped. In one long stride he closed the distance between him and Glines; caught the fat man by the coat-front. Savagely, he slapped the pudgy cheeks—once, twice, three times.

The next instant the guards were upon him—dragging him back, slamming him against the wall.

"Gentlemen!" MacDougal roared. "We'll have no more of this!" His face was beet-red, his blue eyes flashing.

With an effort, Stone slowed his breathing. "Sorry, Mac," he apologized. "I guess I just haven't had enough practice at being called a Communist."

"Nor in curbing your temper, Mr. Stone!" The base director's voice rang ice-brittle. He pivoted to the panting, ruffled Glines. "Mr. Glines, I'd diagnose your aliment as jealousy, pure and simple. If I see any more symtoms of it, it may show up on your efficiency report."

"Yes, sir, Mr. MacDougal." The fat man made jittery motions, smoothing and straightening his coat. "I'm sorry, sir. It won't happen again."

IGNORING him, MacDougal swung back to Stone. "As for you, Carl—well, I'm still in doubt."

"In doubt—?" A cold knot seemed to draw tight in the pit of Stone's stomach. Of a sudden he seemed to sense a change in his friend's manner—a strange, rising tide of latent hostility like that he'd felt in Glines and Bjornberg.

"Yes, in doubt." MacDougal's brows drew together into a shaggy hedgerow. "The dead woman, and this monster business . . . your accusations and violence against Glines, here . . . your expressed fear that Sergeant Bjornberg, one of your best friends on the base, plans to assassinate you—I don't like the sound of such talk."

Stone stood mute, not trusting himself to answer.

"Take your tale about Bjorn-berg," MacDougal went on. "You claim he was on guard outside this building, waiting to kill you. But it so happens that when I called the motor pool for transportation, they sent him to drive me. He'd been there ever since he brought you to this office."

The walls seemed to close in about Stone. He knew every eye in the room was upon him; knew he had to speak. "So—?" he asked at last.

MacDougal paced the floor, big-knuckled hands clasped behind him.

"I don't like to do this, Carl," he said finally, "but considering the delicate nature of our work here, the high degree of secrecy surrounding our mission, I'm afraid I don't have much choice."

The cold knot in Stone's stomach drew tighter.

MacDougal ended his pacing; dropped on one hip on the corner of the desk. His tongue moved slowly back and forth along his lower lip, and his eyes stayed focussed on the floor. When he spoke, his words were careful, casual.

"Did you know we'd acquired a psychiatrist since you left for Washington, Carl?" he asked.

"A psychiatrist—!" Stone burst out in spite of himself. He started forward.

A guard's restraining hand stopped him.

"Yes. She's here on a research project." The base director's eyes still studied the floor. "Supposed to be pretty good, too. Up on all the latest stuff."

Between clenched teeth Stone grated, "MacDougal, if you think I'm crazy, say so. But so help me, if you turn me over to some headshrinker, count on it that you'll regret it to your dying day!"

As if the words were a signal, the base director's massive head came up, jaw jutting. The blue eyes shone hard and expressionless as marbles—shone with the same strange light that Stone had seen in Glines' and Bjornberg's.

MacDougal said, "That's all I needed, Carl: Your threats and hostility turned on me. That's the convincer that you *do* need help."

He turned to the guards: "Mr. Stone's hereby ordered to the hospital for mental tests and observation, on my responsibility.

"Take him away!"

CHAPTER III

DAWN. A chill, grey desert dawn that made Stone shiver beneath his blankets.

Or maybe it wasn't the cold. Maybe it was the things in his mind, the thoughts and nightmares that kept him tossing, twisting, restless. There'd been little enough sleep for him, Lord knew—fitful moments only, from which he started up in wild-eyed terror, racked by aching bones and stinging cuts and the dark uncertainties that wormed insidiously through his brain.

And now, the dawn.

Fretfully, once more he squirmed and shifted—closing his eyes against the dim light, striving to find some new position that would ease the nagging restlessness that plagued him.

But the thin-padded hospital cot only creaked the louder. New lumps and knots created pressure points against his body.

With a curse, he gave it up. Rising, he shrugged on a robe and shuffled to the open window.

If he could call a window open, when it was fitted with a safety screen so heavy that a man with an axe couldn't break through it.

He laugher aloud—short, harsh, without mirth.

Outside, the base still lay bleak and silent, a hollow city with no excuse for being except The Project. The bare, regimented streets stretched deserted between their rows of characterless prefabricated housing. To the south, the tiny airstrip spread desolate, its lone helicopter strangely skeletal at this distance in the chiaroscuro of early morning.

Stone crossed to the other window, the closed one; peered west, towards the bulk of the central Project Building.

The next instant he stiffened.

For where two weeks ago the structure had loomed square and squat, now a tower rose, from its center—a tower somehow disconcertingly unique in styling, not quite like anything he'd ever seen before.

Protuberances of unfathomed purpose marred its symmetry. Catwalks rimmed it at half-a-dozen levels. Even the material of which it was constructed resembled nothing with which he was familiar.

Stoned frowned. True enough, there were plenty of things he didn't know about The Project. That was as it should be, at a base at which security measures were so vital.

Yet at the same time, it seemed strange that he'd have heard no hint as to a construction job of such proportions.

It didn't even fit in with the architectural plans. He'd seen those, and they contained no provision for a tower. None was needed. This was a development base, not a proving ground.

Of course, plans changed. New discoveries and problems necessi-tated new measures, new approaches.

Even new buildings.

The trouble was, so many things seemed to have changed here in the brief span of his fortnight's absence.

The attitudes and atmosphere, for instance. And the people.

People like Bjornberg and Glines and MacDougal.

Or maybe it was he that had changed, the way they said.

Maybe he was really crazy.

He was still brooding about it when the door opened.

The click of the lock took him unawares. There'd been no warning, no sound of footsteps.

Instinctively, he spun about.

Reva stood framed in the doorway.

It rocked him, hard. So hard he could only stand gaping at her cool blonde loveliness, groping for words he couldn't find.

"Good morning, Carl." Her face, her voice, were grave. Briskly, she stepped across the threshold, crisp and neat in a starched white smock, and closed the door behind her.

The spell broke. "Reva—!" he choked. "Reva, what are you doing here?"

Her manner stayed detached, impersonal. "I was assigned here nearly two weeks ago, Carl." And then: "I'm *Doctor* Adams now, you know."

"You mean—you're the psychiatrist?"

She nodded, grey eyes steady. "I'm afraid so, Carl. And I know it's going to be difficult for both of us after the . . . personal . . . relationship. But I didn't have much choice, since I'm the only qualified person here. Mr. MacDougal made that rather plain."

PIN-PRICKS of rising fury seethed through Stone. "You're going along with this farce, then? You'll run me through the mill like any other screwball, in spite of everything—the way it was between us, as close as we were together?" He didn't even care that the words came out thick and angry.

The grey eyes dodged his, now. As if to cover it, Reva moved to the room's lone chair; sat down.

"Answer me!" Stone stormed. "Give it to me straight: Are you going to help them frame me?"

"No one's going to frame you, Carl. It's just that you may be . . . sick. That's all that I'm to check on."

A tremor crept into Reva's voice as she spoke. Hastily, she brought out a pencil and a notebook. "There'll be a few tests, that's all —Minnesota Multiphase Personality, Inventory, Rorschach, TAT, electronencephalogram, in case you're interested in the names. And I'll want to talk to you, of course—discuss these things you've done that seem to bother Mr. MacDougal and the others. There won't be anything unpleasant about it. We can work most of it out over coffee, probably—"

"We'll do it straight, you mean!" Stone clenched his fists, trying to fight down the red tide of rage that surged within him. "Forget your damn' coffee, Doctor Adams! I'm just one more nut to you. Quit trying to hide it!"

Reva's face went stiff. She rose quickly; stood very tall and straight "Very well, then, Carl. We'll handle it just as you prefer. The electroencephalogram comes first. The machine's down at the end of the hall to your right. Just follow me."

High heels clicking, she left the room.

As quickly as it had flared, Stone's fury ebbed. Numbly, he stumbled down the hall after her.

What was it that held him so on edge, so close to the ragged brink of violence? The fight with the monster? The trouble with Bjornberg and Glines and MacDougal? The lack of sleep?

But no. Those were only symptoms of an ever-growing inner tension.

Yet why should he be tense?

He'd seen trouble before—lots of it. Violence, too; blood by the bucket. But it hadn't affected him this way. Through all of it, he'd won a reputation as a man who thrived on situations fraught with worry and frustration. That was why they'd sent him here in the first place, to handle security problems on this base . . .

And to blow up at Reva, still feeling about her as he did . . . to let go at her, when all he could really think of was the hunger in him for her; the desire to take her, hold her, crush her to him . . .

Ahead of him, the heels stopped clicking. Reva pushed open a door; stepped aside. "In here please. Lie down on the couch. I'll attach the electrodes. It won't hurt a bit . . ."

The morning came and went, a jumble of accordian-folded graph sheets and pictures, ink blots and questions. Stone sorted cards, made up stories, drew figures, lay in black silence while electrical impulses eddied through his brain.

There was no coffee, no byplay. Reva stayed Doctor Adams. To the hilt. Lunchtime found Stone alone in his cubicle.

Thirty minutes later they were back at the tests.

But only half Stone's mind was on them.

The other half kept reapprais-ing Reva.

She'd changed, somehow, just like the others. Her impersonality carried a hard, suspicious edge. A dozen times—a hundred—Stone caught her eyes upon him. Not just measuring either: Cold; almost actively hostile.

Especially when she probed him with questions about the woman, and the monster.

LATE afternoon found them in her office, with Reva cross-examining him about his feelings toward Glines and Bjornberg.

The implication was that he'd always hated them both; that the clashes were only the culmination of long-repressed resentment.

Stone's palms grew moist, his heart action uneven.

Of a sudden, he could take no more of it.

"Damn it, Reva!" he exploded. "They jumped me, don't you get it? They started sticking knives in me the second that they saw me!" Vaguely, he was aware that his voice had risen; that he was shouting. He didn't care. "What would you have done, damn it? How would you feel if people accused you of murder and treason to your face, when you'd done noth-ing—?"

He broke off, seething.

The phone rang before Reva

could speak again.

She picked up the receiver, cool and efficient, her eyes still on her notebook. "Doctor Adams speaking." A pause. "No, Mr. MacDougal. I've hardly begun, let alone finished. These things take time." Another pause. "Yes. Yes, I have uncovered a certain amount of pertinent data. But—"

A longer pause. While Stone watched, the smooth planes and curves of Reva's face seemed to stiffen. Her fingers tightened visibly on her pencil, pressing down. The point snapped, loud in the stillness.

She said, "Very well, then, Mr. MacDougal. If you insist.—Yes, I'll be waiting in my office."

She hung up the phone.

Stone smiled thinly. "Report time?"

She didn't answer.

"I know how it is. They always push you." Stone leaned back in his chair. For no good reason, all once he felt more in command of the situation than he had since this whole mad tangle had erupted.

Reva looked away, still saying nothing.

Stone pressed on: "It's too bad things had to work out the way they did . . . Between us."

Reva's eyes stayed on the wall. "We each got what we wanted." Her voice was flat, controlled.

Too tightly controlled.

"Did we?" Stone grimaced. "Maybe you did. I didn't. Because I wanted you. And I didn't get you."

Was it his imagination, or did Reva's breathing quicken just a fraction?

"Being married to a security man's no cinch. I know that. It can get pretty damn' worrisome and lonely, like you said when you broke it off. But right now, I'm wondering if psychiatry can't be lonely, too—"

The mask that was Reva's face drew tighter . . . tighter . . .

"—Especially if you're a woman, Reva—a woman like you, who knows what love is, and needs it—"

In a flash, like an eggshell shattering, the mask cracked and fell apart. Reva turned on him—teeth bared, eyes suddenly streaming. "Shut up!" she screamed. Whiteknuckled, her small fist beat a convulsive tattoo on the desk's polished surface. "Shut up, I tell you! Leave me alone—alone . . . alone . . ."

Her voice died. She slumped on one arm across her notebook, face hidden. The slim shoulders shook with her sobs.

From the office doorway, MacDougal said, "That was dirty, Carl. As dirty as anything you've ever done."

Stone started. Reva gasped aloud and came erect in one swift movement, even as she turned away.

MacDougal stalked heavily to the nearest chair and sat down. Face hewn in granite, he ignored Stone; addressed Reva: "I'm sorry about this, Doctor Adams. Believe me, I wouldn't run you through such a mill for all the world, if it weren't absolutely necessary."

"It's . . . quite all right, Mr. MacDougal." Face almost composed once more, Reva resumed her seat. "I'll give you my tentative report as soon as the attendant returns Mr. Stone to his room." She reached towards a buzzer button.

MacDougal halted her with a gesture. His blue eyes were cold. "Don't bother, Doctor. I'm not inclined to spare Stone's tender feelings, after what he just did to you."

"It's not a matter of feelings, Mr. MacDougal." Abruptly, Reva was very much the doctor. "There's a therapeutic issue involved. And Mr. Stone's my patient."

TIGHT-LIPPED, Stone leaned forward. "Get on with it!" he clipped. "I want to hear what you've got to say as much as he does. If I'm crazy, I've got a right to know it."

" 'Crazy' is hardly a meaningful term, medically speaking, Mr. Stone." Reva stared down at her notes. "However, if you insist. . ."

"I do."

"Very well, then." She turned to MacDougal; tapped an accordian-folded graph on the desk. "Are you familiar with electroencephalography, Mr. MacDougal?"

The base director shrugged. "Only vaguely."

"Then let me begin by expaining that the electroencephalograph is a device which measures currents within the brain and records them on a chart. A trained technician can then interpret the patterns in diagnostic terms."

"I see."

"In Mr. Stone's case"—Reva studied the chart—"the electroencephalogram shows marked deviation from the norm. I'm inclined to believe that the pattern indicates he's a victim of epidemic encephalitis."

"Encephalitis—?" MacDougal frowned. "I'm afraid you'll have to explain, Doctor. I've never heard of it."

Reva nodded gravely. "That's not surprising, sir. No acute cases have been reported since 1925. The ones we see today are chronic—the aftermath of an epidemic that swept the country, beginning in 1919."

"And the results?"

"That all depends." Reva sketched meaningless patterns with her pencil. "You see, the disease wreaks havoc in the brain. There's tissue damage and, later, of course, residual lesions. Ganglion cells and neurons degenerate or disappear. Behavior difficulties often follow, too—chronic irritability, emotional instability, psychopathic conduct."

"You tell it scary," Stone said tightly. "There's just one catch, though: So far as I know, I never had any such disease."

Reva didn't look up. "I'm afraid that's easily possible, Carl. It may have run concurrently with influenza or some other sickness. Plenty of cases weren't detected. But the damage still was done."

"Then how is it I've survived? Why haven't they carted me off before now?"

"Because of the nature of the disease, Carl." For the first time, Reva faced him squarely. "You see, it can become progressive, even after months and years. When that happens . . ." Helplessly, she spread her hands.

A numbness crept through Stone. He slumped in his chair. The room seemed to grow dim around him. He hardly heard the things the other two were saying.

Was this to be the end for him, then? Must he live out his life walled away from the world in some mental hospital?

Again, he lived through the night before . . . tried to recall the way he'd felt, the things he'd done.

He'd been tired, yes; but that was to be expected, what with the long trip in. And his spirits had certainly been good enough.

Then he'd seen the woman . . . fought the monster.

And whether anyone believed him or not, the battle had been reality, not delusion. He had the scars to prove it.

Chronic irritability? Emotional instability? Psychopathic conduct? Those were terms that fitted Bjornberg and Glines better than they did him.

Though he had to admit he'd been on the jumpy side, ever since he'd reached the base.

Ever since he'd reached the base—!

With a rush, the pieces fell into pattern.

Last night, he'd fought a monster—a creature like nothing ever seen on earth, in hell or heaven.

The dying woman had gasped of robots on a mesa.

Bjornberg had accused him of murder.

Glines had sworn he was a Communist.

MacDougal had ordered him

checked for mental aberration.

An unscheduled, other-worldish tower had risen atop the Project Building.

Reva had diagnosed him as an encephalitic, fully capable of psychopathic conduct and suitable for confinement.

He himself had developed a sudden tension so nerve-shattering as to make him question his own sanity.

It all added up to just one thing: Something horribly dangerously wrong.

But not with him. No.

With the base!

But what? What could possibly account for such mad deviation?

HE looked up sharply. Reva was still talking:

"—so after your description of Carl's behavior, Mr. MacDougal, my first thought was paranoia. The systematized delusions and hallucinations tied in with it, and so did his tendency to violence. But I've given him the Rorschach test, and the TAT, and neither of them show any indication of it. So tentatively, I'm forced to fall back on encephalitis. It manifests itself so many ways—it's more polymorphic than syphilis, even . . ."

Systematized delusions—? Hallucinations? Stone felt a sudden, quick twinge of excitement. The be-

havior of the people here on the base fitted that pattern.

Yet how could a whole organization turn paranoid?

Besides, Reva had just said that he himself didn't check out for it on the tests.

Thoughtfully, he studied her.

She knew about these things, these mental twists, and she'd just come here.

Could the trouble be some strange infection she'd brought with her?

For that matter, why would a psychiatrist be assigned to a development base, anyhow?

It was an interesting question. Spontaneously, he cut in on the conversation: "Reva . . ."

She looked around. "Yes, Carl?"

"Just what is this research project of yours?"

Her face froze, lips half-parted. The grey eyes—it was as if shutters had suddenly slammed closed behind them.

Cold, hostile shutters.

MacDougal said quickly, "I'm afraid we'll have to bounce that one, Carl. *Verboten*. Doctor Adams' work is classified, highly confidential."

Ice hung on his words—the same kind of ice that glazed Reva's eyes.

And Glines'. And Bjornberg's.

Stone held his face immobile. "Sorry. I didn't know."

Reva had come here. Strange things had happened.

Reva was a psychiatrist. Base personnel showed something close to mental disorder.

Cause and effect?

It could bear some thought. Quite a bit of thought, in fact. Not to mention thorough investigation.

MacDougal's blue eyes had narrowed. Abruptly, he turned to Reva. "Doctor Adams, I'm afraid I've imposed on you. It's not fair to ask you to treat patients, in addition to your . . . other work."

Reva's slim shoulders moved a fraction. "I admit the facilities are hardly adequate, Mr. MacDougal."

"Then you recommend a mental hospital?"

"I'm afraid so."

"We'll have him flown out tonight in the helicopter, then. Right now." The base director surged to his feet. "Let's go, Carl."

Stone gripped the arms of his chair.

One wrong question—and in seconds they'd arranged to put him out of circulation.

Which meant he'd been right: There *was* a relationship between Reva's coming, her work, and the changes on the base.

Only a lot of good knowing it would do him, locked away in a back ward of some asylum. Even if he was actually all right it would take months to convince the doctors.

So much for his plans.

Unless—

"Hurry it up, Carl. This is all for your own good, you know."

Wordless, Stone arose. Carefully casual, he glanced out the nearest window.

It was almost dark.

So much the better.

He moved on into the hall and shuffled towards the detention room where he'd spent the night. Reva and MacDougal followed.

The door was locked. Stone stood aside, waiting loose-muscled while Reva inserted the key and opened the door.

"I won't keep you waiting long, Carl," MacDougal said. "We'll pick you up just as soon as I locate a pilot."

Stone drew a deep breath, "Any time." He started forward.

The base director shifted aside to let him pass.

Stone smashed down his foot with all his might on the other's instep.

MacDougal cried out . . . tottered off-balance.

Twisting, Stone shoved him hard against Reva. Together, the pair sprawled on the floor of the detention room.

Stone slammed and locked the door behind them. It muffled their cries most satisfactorily.

Bleak-eyed, then, he strode down the corridor and the stairs and out into the night . . .

CHAPTER IV

BASE Directory Service gave Stone both Reva's addresses— her prefab, and the building assigned her for her project.

Hanging up the phone, he pushed his way out of the crowded drugstore, then stood hesitating on the curb of the broad, bright-lighted parkway that ran round the parking center.

Home, or office? Which should it be?

He frowned.

The base alarm system blasted in the same instant.

The noisy crowd fell suddenly silent. People paused, fell back a step. Eyes shifted, searched.

The siren's shrill scream died away.

Ripples of apprehension rose on its echo. Little groups drew close together, milling aimlessly.

A tiny chill ran through Stone. He had no choice now. Distance was the vital factor, and the office address was the closest.

With an effort, he held his steps even and unhurried. Crossing the parkway, he headed south on the nearest street.

All about him, men and women were emptying from the prefabs— peering this way and that talking excitedly. Off to the right, out by the Project Building motor pool, a jeep's lights flashed on. A gunned motor roared. The lights swerved north as the vehicle raced away.

Seconds later, another followed. Then another, and another.

Elsewhere, in all directions, other motors droned as the base security system came to life.

The chase was on.

Stone veered between the buildings, out of sight, then broke into a dog-trot.

A cross-street. Pausing in the shadows, he strained his eyes against the night, searching both ways for signs of the blockade the jeeps were setting up, according to plan.

It was a good plan, too; he'd helped devise it. Once the vehicles reached their stations, a rabbit couldn't move across the base undetected.

After that, there'd be a block-check, certain capture.

But until then—He strode across the street, not too fast till again he reached the welcoming shadows. There, once in the darkness, he broke into a pelting run.

More cross-streets; more speed.

Then the last line of prefabs.

Beyond them spread the dim expanse of the Related Projects Area, with its high wire fence and guarded gates.

Stone halted, breathing hard, and smoothed his shirt and combed his hair. Then, boldly, he strode towards the nearest point of entry.

The guard on the gate watched through the mesh, cold-eyed and silent, as he approached.

Stone said, "Message for Doctor Coughlin, Materials Research. Here's my pass."

He extended his wallet as he spoke. Cradling his rifle, the guard unlatched the gate and reached out to take it.

Stone smashed the free-swinging gate violently against him.

The guard lurched back; tried to jerk up his rifle.

Side-stepping, Stone lunged in close. Savagely, he hammered an uppercut to the other's jaw.

The guard dropped.

Ripping the man's shirt into strips, Stone bound and gagged him in seconds. Then, snatching up the rifle, he ran for the shadows.

The small, one-story brick building that housed Reva's project stood apart from its fellows, far back in an isolated corner of the Related Projects Area. A steel framework like a miniature radio tower rose close beside it, perhaps fifty feet tall.

Smashing open the locked door with the rifle-butt, Stone snapped on the lights and surveyed the place.

THE room in which he stood was a typical office. Filing cases banked one wall. A desk flanked by bookshelves stood against a second. There was a long table littered with papers and, incongruously, a small bowl of flowers. Three chairs, a water cooler, and a coatrack completed the furnishings.

Hurriedly, Stone crossed to the nearest of the two inside doors.

The first led to a washroom.

The second was locked.

Stone hesitated, a vague uneasiness upon him. It was as if the tension that rode him had been suddenly, sharply heightened. His muscles ached; his fingers showed a tendency to tremble.

The humming impinged on him, then.

It was as vague as his uneasiness —a sound that was not a sound, almost.

Stone turned slowly—straining his ears; trying to trace the murmur to its source.

Finally he placed it: It centered on the door beside which he stood.

He swung the rifle-butt. Once—twice—three times.

Lock and door stood fast.

Once again Stone hesitated. Then, reversing the rifle and standing aside to avoid a ricochet, he triggered a shot at the lock.

Metal jangled through the echo. Another blow with the butt, and the door creaked open.

The windowless room beyond, from its cramped size, had probably been planned primarily for storage.

Now, though, it overflowed with electronic equipment, from floor to ceiling a buzzing maze of tubes and condensers and coils and complicated circuits such as Stone had never seen before.

Could this machine be responsible for his uneasiness and the strange behavior on the base?

There was one sure way to find out.

Narrow-eyed, nerves atingle, he pivoted, searching for the master switch . . . located it at last, set at the far end of the narrow space between a transformer and the wall.

He reached out; gripped the shiny black handle.

Then, before he could throw it, a harsh voice from the office behind him snarled, "Move an inch and you're dead!"

Stone went rigid.

"Now come out! On the double!"

Stone's spine tingled. He let go

the switch and slowly turned.

Colt in hand, hard-eyed and lethal, Sergeant Bjornberg stood hunched in a gunman's crouch on the far side of the office.

Glines flanked him.

Stone's lips felt stiff. Of a sudden he could feel death's hand on his shoulder.

Bjornberg moved a quick step forward. "Come out, I said!"

The smirk on Glines' fat face would have fitted a cat better. A well-fed cat, toying with a mouse.

Stone sucked in air.

"What's the matter, Mr. Stone?" It was Glines talking now—sneering, mocking. "You took a gun away from me last night. Why don't you take the sergeant's?"

"Shut up!" rasped Bjornberg. And then, to Stone: "I said come out! Away from that equipment!"

'Away from that equipment . . .'

Ever so slowly, Stone let out the deep breath he'd been holding. "No, thanks, Sergeant."

"What—!" Bjornberg's finger went white on the trigger.

STONE smiled stiffly. "I said no, Joe. I'd rather let you shoot—because whether you hit me or not, that forty-five's going to tear up a lot of transistors."

Bjornberg's mouth worked. "Damn you, Stone!" And Glines came in high and shrill. "You should have hit him with the barrel from behind, Sergeant! You shouldn't have warned him!"

Ever so casually, Stone leaned back against the framework of the machine.

"I'll still take him!" Bjornberg snarled. "Here, cover me!"

He passed the Colt to Glines and started forward, hands raised in a judo fighter's guard.

Stone lunged for the switch.

This time, there was no turning back, no hesitation. He slammed the black handle down even as Bjornberg crashed against him.

The humming died in a click of circuit breakers. The tubes began to dim.

Twisting, too cramped to strike a blow, Stone grappled with Bjornberg. Together, they rocked back to the far side of the doorway, fighting with knees and teeth and elbows.

Then the sergeant broke free; leaped back, out into the office.

Instead of trying to follow, Stone spun about and smashed his foot through a device that looked like an off-beat magnetron. Clutching whole handfuls of wiring, he tore one of the upper racks of equipment out bodily.

Then Bjornberg was upon him again. The man's weight hammered him down. He caught a wicked blow in the back of the neck that sent him sagging to his knees on the floor.

Now a fist jarred his head back. Desperately, he caught one of Bjornberg's ankles and wrenched it up and around, twisting with savage force.

It was the sergeant's turn to crash to the floor. Rolling clear of him, Stone scrambled to his feet.

His adversary did likewise.

Then, as they started to circle, each searching for an opening, a voice cut through: "Carl! Sergeant! Stop it!" It was Glines, almost shouting. "Stop it, I tell you! Stop it!"

Wary, still gasping for breath, Stone drew back.

It was only then that it came to him, dazedly, that the strange tension he'd felt for the past twenty-four hours had left him. In spite of Bjornberg's blows, his head seemed clearer than it had been since the night before. His muscles no longer ached with strain. His hands had lost their tendency to tremble.

Instead of all such, now, an intense, overwhelming weariness hung upon him; nothing more.

Across from him, Bjornberg shook his head jerkily, as if to clear his brain. The hard lines had vanished from his face. Suspicion clouded his eyes no longer. They were open now, wide open, frank and friendly the way Stone had always known them.

Over by the desk, Glines shifted awkwardly, the Colt forgotten on the floor beside him. His mouth hung loose, and he looked stunned, incredulous—a fat, good-natured little man with just a bit of the old maid in him. "Carl," he mumbled, swabbing perspiration from his forehead, "Carl, what have I been doing?"

Bjornberg broke in: "Did I really say you killed that woman, Carl? My God, I must have been crazy!"

Of a sudden Stone's legs were weak as water. He stumbled to the nearest chair; slumped in it.

"This whole base has been crazy," he grunted.

Glines' pudgy hands moved nervously. He groped: "But how—I mean, what happened—?"

"It was driven crazy, that's what happened," Stone said tightly. He jerked a thumb over his shoulder. "That machine in there did it."

"The machine—?" This from Bjornberg. His broad brow wrinkled. "I thought it was a project—"

"And you thought it was important too, didn't you? Important enough to kill me for?"

The sergeant's face grew red. He shifted from one foot to the other. "I guess I did, Carl. Only now—well—damn it, I'm all mixed up!"

"Who isn't?" Stone turned to Glines. "How'd you feel—last night, when you heard about me, I mean?"

THE fat man squirmed. "It's— Carl, I don't know how to tell you . . ." He chewed his puffy lower lip. "As well as I can remember, I'd been feeling tight and jittery for a long time—a week or more. Then, when the sergeant woke me up and told me about you—and that dead woman—and your story about the monster—well, it was strange. All at once I was angry. I hated you, and I was afraid of you, somehow. I kept remembering all kinds of little things, and by the time I got to the office I—I knew you were a Communist. I *knew* it." Nervously, again he swabbed his forehead, scarlet now as Bjornberg's. "I hope you understand, Carl; I just can't explain it."

"I understand, all right," Stone said grimly. "The trouble is, I can't explain it either. Not all of it. Not the important parts."

"But the machine, you said—"

"Sure, the machine did it. But why?" Stone leaned forward. "Look: First of all, somebody had to design it. Then somebody else had to approve it, order it built. Why?"

Glines shook his head helplessly. Bjornberg stared at the floor.

Stone pressed on: "Second, it didn't seem to cause any trouble—outside of making everybody jittery—till I came along. But when I did, everybody went haywire. Except me. Or maybe I did, too. Maybe I didn't really fight a monster.

"But I think I did, and I've got some scars to prove it. So that brings up a third point: Why didn't it throw me, like it did the rest of you? How is it I could figure out that something was wrong on the base, and that this project was responsible, when nobody else could?"

"It's crazy, just crazy, that's all," muttered Bjornberg.

"Maybe. But I doubt it." Stone rose stiffly. "There's somebody I want to ask some questions—" He stopped short. "Tell me this: How'd you happen to come here looking for me?"

Glines frowned. "That was my idea, Carl. Mr. MacDougal sent for me after he and Doctor Adams finally got out of that room at the hospital and sounded the alarm for you. He asked me if I had any idea where you might go—after all, I'd worked with you for a long time. At first I said I didn't know. Only then Doctor Adams made some remark about your—your condition, and said she hoped you wouldn't twist your delusions of persecution around to where you'd try to do something to her, like you'd done to that dead woman. Mr. MacDougal said she didn't need to worry about it, that he'd see that she got home all right, and they left. But the more I thought about what she'd said, the more sense it made, and I began to wonder if you might not try to sneak out here and booby-trap the building. Finally, the thought of it got to worrying me so much that I called Sergeant Bjornberg and came out here with him." Glines paused, laughed self-consciously. "It sounds silly now, doesn't it? But at the time nothing in the world seemed so important as to make sure nothing happened to Doctor Adams or her project."

Reva. Always, it came back to Reva.

"Good enough," Stone said. Tight-lipped, he started for the door.

"Where you going?" Bjornberg demanded.

Stone held his voice flat and level. "To see Doctor Adams."

"That figures," the sergeant nodded. "We even got a jeep back by the next building to take you to her."

"Besides," Glines chimed in, opening the door, "you'll need us to pass you through the blockade."

He started down the outside

steps.

The next instant, his wild scream of terror split the night.

CHAPTER V

FOR Stone, that moment lasted a thousand years.

Then it was over, Glines' shriek dying.

The horrid spell broke. He lunged for the door, Bjornberg on his heels.

But something smooth and slippery brushed his face as he crossed the threshold. Instinctive panic flaring in him, he threw himself sidewise.

Before he could hit the ground, rubbery tentacles swept about him. In a black delirium of movement, he found himself caught up and lifted; crushed close to a gelid, barrel-like body.

Desperately, he tried to twist free, fight clear. But a dozen discs clung to him with vicious suction. Every move he made seemed to draw the tentacles tighter—crushing him; squeezing the very breath from his body.

Now one had looped about his throat, a living rope to cut the blood off from his brain. Glines' screams seemed dim and far away. The sky held too many stars.

Then thunder rocked the night— the thunder of a heavy Colt, fired at close range.

For the fraction of a second, the tentacles' hold relaxed. Stone's feet touched the ground. Tearing his throat free, he gulped in a tremendous, sobbing breath.

"Joe!" he shouted. "Joe, shoot for the band, the belt—"

Nightmare-like, in the same instant the tentacles once again constricted. He had no more breath— not for shouting, nor for breathing either.

But the Colt roared like an echo, so close now that the powder-fumes stung Stone's nostrils. The monster's barrel-body rocked under hammer-blows of impact. Fluid spilled across Stone's legs in a chilling gush.

Then he was free, falling, slammed to the gravel. Tentacles writhed across him in a rush.

Rolling, Stone lurched up.

The monster that had held him now clutched Bjornberg. In a raging frenzy, its tentacles swung the sergeant high into the air wrenching at his body. His head lolled— loose, horribly disjointed.

Then, with cataclysmic violence, the thing hurled him from it. He crashed against the brick wall of the building; spilled down in a crumpled heap beside a sodden form that could only be Glines' body.

Stone turned and ran.

Ahead of him, a second monster swept out from behind the building.

Stone kept to his course, straight at the thing. If asked, he could not have told why. Perhaps it was bravado, perhaps desperation.

Or perhaps pure madness.

The creature hesitated, its tentacles flickering in a way that was almost startled. Then, abruptly, it drew back, as if suddenly wary —not quite certain of Stone's potential.

Beyond it, the jeep loomed. Stone made it in a final rush; vaulted into the driver's seat. Kicking the motor to life, he wheeled the vehicle around in a screaming curve, jammed the accelerator to the floor, and raced for the main gate.

In seconds, the entrance came into view. Stone started to apply the brakes.

But the gate stood open. No guards appeared to challenge his exit.

Beyond the fence, the street stretched bare and empty, with no sign of blockading troops.

Stone bore down on the gas once more. He still didn't dare to pause to think; not yet. The horror still clung too close. Too many things hung unexplained.

Things like why the firing back at Reva's project building hadn't drawn a half-track full of guards.

Why the gate stood open. Why the streets were empty, the housing units dark.

But such were trivia; they could wait. He only knew his friends were dead, and what he had to do.

Number Ten Q Street, Northeast. Reva's prefab.

But no light in the windows.

STONE spun the jeep right at the next corner; headed back west towards the Central Project Building, with its bright lights and strange new tower.

Then, ahead, a white-striped barrier caught his lights. It blocked the street.

Stone braked the jeep.

Half-a-dozen soldiers stood grouped to one side of the crossbar. Before Stone could even speak, two of them hurriedly slung their rifles, moved the barrier out of the way, and waved him on. They made no move to halt or check him.

The area beyond looked like a full-scale military operation—barricades, barbed wire, sandbagged strong points, machine guns.

Hands slick on the jeep's wheel, still not daring to ask questions, Stone maneuvered his vehicle through the narrow corridor left open.

He reached the fence that circled the Central Project Area . . . passed through the gate.

On the other side, thronging civilians milled and muttered. A single word, rising from a thousand throats, pulsed at him wave-like:

"Monsters . . . monsters . . . monsters . . . monsters. . ."

Of a sudden, Stone understood it all—the barricades, the darkened houses; the open gates, the lack of questions.

New chills ran through him. He cursed the icy sweat that drenched his body.

Slowed .by the crowd, the jeep was more hindrance now than help. Abandoning it, Stone pushed his way towards the square, squat block of the Central Project Building.

A private with rifle and fixed bayonet barred the entrance. A corporal sang out. "Hold it, Mister!"

Stone said tightly, "You hold it —if you want to take the responsibility. I've got information about this business."

A lieutenant moved up. "Talk ahead, Mister. I'll listen."

"I'll talk—to the base director. And he's the only one."

The lieutenant's eyes narrowed. "What's your name, Mister?"

"Carl Stone."

"Carl Stone—!" Visibly, the officer stiffened. He shoved the private aside; elbowed back the corporal. "Come on, then! What are you waiting for?"

In seconds, they were at the door of MacDougal's second-floor office.

The base director sat hunched over his desk, snapping hard, clipped words into a phone. His broad face looked drawn and haggard, and the hand with which he pushed back his stiff, greying hair seemed not too steady.

Stone's gaze flicked to Reva Adams.

She occupied a chair in one corner. Only in the faint shadows beneath her eyes did she show any trace of the tension that radiated from the base director. For the rest, she was as always—sleek, lovely, all woman, her blonde hair swept smoothly back and falling to her shoulders, her firm body filling out the silken sheath of her dress.

Even the sight of her sent fury surging through Stone. Pushing past the lieutenant, he stalked into the room. "Hang up that phone, Mac. You've got company."

Reva jerked in her chair. Her hand flew to her throat.

Th base director's massive head came around sharply. He started up from his seat. "Carl—!"

"Right. Alive and breathing." There was no good humor in the words, the way Stone said them. He heeled shut the door, closing out the lieutenant.

"Carl, we thought you were

dead—"

"I'm not blaming you, Mac. Not you." Stone jerked his head towards Reva. "Her, I'm not so sure of."

"Doctor Adams—?" MacDougal stared at him blankly. "What do you mean, Carl?"

"I mean I've found out the nature of her project." Grimly, Stone pivoted to face the woman. "How about it, Reva? What's the explanation for that electronic brain-trap I found out in your building?"

Her slim hands moved nervously in her lap. Her eyes dodged his. "I—I don't know what you mean."

"You don't?" Stone made an elaborate business of surprise. And then, slashing out, hard and savage: "I'll tell *you*, then. I'm talking about that transmitter you had locked in your storeroom—that humming, buzzing little devil-machine that kept this whole base half-crazy till I smashed it!"

MacDougal's heavy fist hammered on the desk. "Damn it, Carl! Talk sense!"

"I am talking sense—the only sense anybody's heard around here in the past two weeks!" Stone roared him down. "Has it occurred to you that you feel a little differently about me now than you did a couple of hours ago?"

THE base director suddenly looked sheepish. "Oh, that—" He groped vaguely. "I—well, I don't know what got into me, Carl. Nervous strain, maybe. The pressure of sweating out the big project, here; all the worry, the being afraid it wouldn't work out right . . ."

"And then, awhile ago, all of a sudden you knew that it was foolish, didn't you? That I wasn't crazy, or a traitor, or a murderer, or anything else except what I'd always been?"

"Well—well, yes." MacDougal brushed perspiration from his chin. "As soon as I got back here, and stopped to think it over—"

"You mean, as soon as I smashed that machine! Bjornberg, Glines —they both snapped out of the fog when I did it, right before my eyes."

"Glines? Bjornberg?" MacDougal's head came up. "I've had a call out for them. Where are they?"

Tight-lipped, Stone fought down the wave of sickness that rose in him. "They're dead, Mac. Dead. Killed by the monsters that everybody claimed I didn't see."

"Dead. . ." Face sagging, the base director slumped into his chair.

"I'm as sorry as you are, Mac. But that's not enough." Stone pushed in, driving his words hard. "What's important is now, the living. They're the ones we've got to think about."

"Yes. Of course." MacDougal's voice still echoed dull and empty.

"So the first point's to get it across that I'm not crazy, that I'm telling the truth: Last night, that transmitter out at Reva's building wouldn't let you believe me. Then, when I smashed it, and everybody snapped back to normal, the monsters came—so many of them that you've had to clear the base, move all personnel into the Central Project Area for protection."

"But how—?"

"How do the monsters tie in with the transmitter, you mean?" Stone shook his head curtly. "I wouldn't know. But I'm going to find out. Our good friend Doctor Adams is going to tell us all about it."

He turned towards her chair.

It was empty.

Stone went numb inside; spun about by reflex.

The office door stood an inch ajar. Reva was gone.

MacDougal cursed, surged up from his seat. "Come on!" Like a raging grizzly, he charged across the office and out into the hall.

Stone started to follow. Then, braking, he whirled and jumped to the window. Savagely, he jerked it open and thrust out his head.

Off to the right, below him, Reva was walking briskly out the building's main entrance, a picture of calm, cool poise.

Stone clutched the sill; looked down.

A soldier wearing an MP brassard stood directly beneath him. Stone shouted, "You, soldier! MP! Get that woman!"

The man looked up, startled; then to the right, following Stone's frantic gesture.

But the words had reached Reva, too. She swung round in mid-stride, her eyes wide with panic.

The MP galloped towards her.

Whirling, she fled right—away from her pursuer; off towards the corner of the building.

Stone ran for the hall, only to crash into MacDougal, returning.

The base director's face was flushed. He was panting. "I couldn't find her, Carl—"

"Forget it. She's trapped. Just wait in your office." Stone headed for the stairs at a dead run.

Outside at last, then, he spotted the MP.

The man waved and gestured.

Stone went limp with relief. The soldier had Reva gripped firmly by the arm.

Stone started towards them.

Only then, suddenly, out in the open area in front of the building, a civilian gave a startled cry and pointed skyward.

Simultaneously, a high, shrill

drone pulsed through the night, louder every second.

Stone looked up sharply.

OVERHEAD, pinpoints of light were sweeping down in tight formation, coverging on the Central Project Area. Lower they raced, and lower, wheeling in a spiral that would have been the envy of any jet.

Out in the crowd, a woman screamed hysterically. A man whirled, sprinting for cover.

In an instant, panic swept through the multitude like a living thing. Shrieking, bolting, clawing, civilians and soldiers alike fled in all directions.

Heart pounding, Stone pressed flat against the building.

Now one of the lights peeled off from the formation. Bullet-fast, it lanced towards the spot where Stone stood, so low that it almost seemed to skim the ground.

He drew a quick, shallow breath, with the feeling that it must surely be his last.

Only then the thing spun into an arc, bare yards away from him. For an instant it hovered almost motionless, barely three feet in the air, before riding a beam of purple flame from its base down to the ground.

Stone could see it better now. A tripod of tall, thin metal legs supported a blocky central unit that vaguely resembled a cake ice-cream cup with a broad lip flaring at the top, Light glinted from three eye-like protuberances set close against the brim.

While Stone watched, the purple beam that speared down from the center of the body unit turned scarlet, then dazzling pink. At the same time, two funnel-shaped appendages detached themselves from the base and darted out, cobra-like, in either direction along the building's wall on slender tentacles of cable.

Off to Stone's right, a shout rang out. Then a shot.

He turned just in time to glimpse the tentacle flick out like a whip-lash at the MP who'd captured Reva. Its funnel-shaped end struck him in the chest—a blow so violent that even Stone could hear it hit.

The man staggered back; sank to the ground.

Paying him no heed, the cable flipped high into the air, coiling as it rose.

Then, writhing like a living thing, it was descending . . . slapping down at Reva Adams.

Her scream rang wild and ragged. Like one possessed, she darted out from the building, blonde hair streaming.

Deftly, the cable-coil shifted,

pulling tight even as it dropped its loop around her.

Tripping, she plunged to the ground.

In spite of himself, without volition, Stone lunged towards her. Unreasoning panic roweled him with razor spurs.

Almost as if timing itself to his charge, the cable-tentacle threw another loop around the struggling woman, then swept her high into the air above Stone's head just as he reached the spot where she had lain.

Desperately, he leaped straight up, clawing for the cable.

Snake-like, it writhed out of reach, leaving him to fall back cursing on the gravel.

Now he saw the other tentacle's destination.

And its victim.

It was MacDougal.

The funnel-like cable-end had suckered onto his great chest and dragged him bodily out his office window. Now, still at second-story level, heedless of his struggles, the line itself twisted and looped about him half-a-dozen times, binding him tight.

Simultaneously, the flame-jet from the strange robot's base deepened to its original purple.

As the color changed, the weird craft lifted, higher into the air, and higher. Already, it had begun to pick up its characteristic spiral motion.

In the same instant, the other robots swept down, still in their tight formation. The shrill drone of the sound they gave forth welled ear-splitting, deafening.

Smoothly, the unit that had landed resumed its place within the pattern, its sagging prisoners hugged against it.

As one, the robots soared away, out across the encircling desert till light and sound alike were swallowed in the night.

CHAPTER VI

THE moment that followed the flying robots' departure stretched endlessly, Seconds ticked by with Stone barely aware that they were passing. He could only stand there in mute, helpless frustration, staring up at the sky where the cones had vanished.

Out of the night they had come; into that same night they had retreated.

Only there was more to it than that.

Because they'd taken Reva and MacDonald with them. That, obviously, had been the whole purpose of their raid.

Nor had their victims gone willingly. No one who had seen those blanched, fear-stricken faces could believe they had.

No. If there'd been a plot—if Reva had really helped the monsters by setting up the transmitter at her project building—then that plot had now reversed itself, gone sour.

It was a mad twist—shattering; mind-shaking.

And it forced a whole new orientation.

For Stone, it was suddenly more than he could take or grasp. He slumped against the wall; buried his face in his hands.

Then, from all directions, sound rose and swept in and impinged upon him—a hoarse babble of voices that echoed overtones of panic.

He let his hands fall; looked up and out.

The teeming mass of humanity crammed into Central Project Area seethed like churned water. Shouts of rage rang out . . . roars of indignation, women's high-voice protests, the fear-straught cries of frightened children.

While Stone watched, the troops drew in to form a tight, bayonet-bristling cordon about the Project Building, thrusting the civilians back.

Numb, drained, Stone turned from the scene and made his way to the main entrance.

A half-track stood drawn up close by it, with a lieutenant colonel barking orders into a radio-phone. Pausing, Stone listened long enough to ascertain that the man was talking to the commander of an armored unit on maneuver somewhere out in the desert—calling it in to reenforce the troops stationed at the base in case of further robot raids or incursions by the monsters.

Chaos, Unlimited.

Shaking his head wearily, Stone went on into the building and headed for the first-floor snack bar.

The place was deserted, save for a little knot of research men who sat talking animatedly at a table beside a blaring radio at the far end of the room.

In spite of himself, Stone's lips twisted wryly. Leave it to Research. Let Earth itself collapse, and its intellectual stalwarts would still forget panic in their eagerness to argue the dynamics of the break-up.

The girl at the coffee urn gave him a wan smile. "Coffee, Mr. Stone?"

"Jug of black," Stone grunted. "I need something to help me do some thinking."

STILL talking, two of the research men came up behind him while he waited.

". . . that confounded tower,

that's what gets me," the first was saying. "With MacDougal gone, what do we do about it?"

"Then what Crawford said's true? Nobody except MacDougal actually knows the purpose of it?"

"You're so right. I was there when he gave the orders on it, a week-and-a-half ago. He was so excited he could hardly keep his pants on; but when Grimorski asked him what the idea was, he just stuck out his eyebrows and told Grim to mind his own business."

The second man whistled. "It puts us on a spot, then, doesn't it?"

"Spot's hardly the name for it. That tower doesn't tie in with The Project at all, except maybe for using some of the big equipment."

The girl at the coffee urn handed Stone his cup and jug. Mechanically, he took them, paid her, and stepped back out of the way of the research men.

But his mind was racing, groping. He made no move to find a table.

"One with cream and one without," the second research man told the girl. And then, speaking again to his companion: "I was talking to Santos about it. He says the only thing he can figure it for is some kind of king-size electrolytic cracker. Only it's too big to make sense, and it'd have to work on

some off-beat principle that doesn't tie in with accepted theories on ionization."

"Even if it did, what would the monstrosity decompose? The atmosphere?" This from the first man. "No; I can't buy that, Dawes. If you ask me, it doesn't do anything at all."

"Oh, now, don't push those snap judgments of yours too far, Quinn." The second man looked half-worried, half-amused. "After all, why would MacDougal order the thing built, if it didn't have some function?"

"What's the obvious answer?" the man called Quinn snorted. "Our base director's cracked, that's all. The strain got too much for him. He saw how things were going on The Project—that it just wasn't going to work out, even if it was his idea and his baby. He simply couldn't take it. So, he compensated by coming up with a new super-secret brainstorm that's as nutty as a Rube Goldberg invention."

The other research man frowned. "You really think so?"

"What else is there to think? Can you come up with any other explanation?"

"But MacDougal — damn it, Quinn, he's outstanding, brilliant —"

"The smarter they are, the wider

they split. It's happened before. A man stakes his career on a job; oversells an idea. Then it falls flat. He sees his whole scientific reputation flying out the window. Unless he's mighty stable, the next stop's Bellevue."

Cups in hand, the two research men started to move away, back to their table.

For the fraction of a second, Stone hesitated. Then, abruptly, he stepped forward. "Pardon me . . ."

The pair halted. The first man half-turned. "What—?"

Stone said, "I'm Carl Stone. Security. I couldn't help overhearing—"

The second man flinched visibly, slopping his coffee. His thin face paled a trifle.

His companion stood steady. "Go ahead." His voice was cool, not too friendly.

Stone made a placatory gesture. "Believe me, I'm not trying to give you trouble. There'll be no nonsense about reporting anybody, no matter what. But some strange things have happened on this base lately. I need information—and maybe you two are the ones who can give it to me." He nodded to the nearest table. "How about letting me have five minutes, over coffee?"

"I've got nothing to hide. What I said's for the record." The first man stepped to the table, dropped into a chair.

The second followed, less enthusiastically.

STONE filled his cup from the jug and leaned back, hunting for the right words. "You think there's a possibility that The Project's a failure?" he asked finally.

"Possibility, my eye. It's a thousand per cent certain." The first man, the one called Quinn, stirred in sugar. "Has been, for nearly a month now. But MacDougal won't give up. Because he doesn't know it? No; it's because he's scared to."

Stone frowned at Dawes. "You agree?"

The man stared down into his coffee. "I'm afraid so."

"Then why hasn't it been reported—to Washington, I mean?"

"That's—that's the base director's responsibility."

"And this other business? The tower?" Stone spoke to Quinn, this time.

"You've got me there, mister." The man made a business of shrugging. "I've screamed loud enough about it, but no one would listen. I guess they think griping's just a habit with me, on account of my encephalitis."

Stone stiffened. ."*Encephalitis*

—?"

"A brain disease. I picked it up in the flu epidemic of 1918, when I was a kid. Doesn't bother my thinking, but I'll admit it short-circuits my disposition sometimes."

"So—"—with difficulty, Stone held his voice level—"so, you didn't think much of the tower?"

"That's right. I didn't. But everyone else was so hipped on it they wouldn't listen—even Dawes, here, had the bug. For better than a week, they all went around acting like it was the hottest thing since blondes were invented, and the most important, even when in the next breath they'd have to admit they didn't know what it was supposed to do or how it worked. I was the only one in the place who wouldn't join their club. I think they'd have fired me, if they'd had a replacement. As it was, the supervisor just swore I was crazy and let it go at that."

"I see." Stone gripped his cup between his palms, trying to hide his hands' sudden trembling.

Slowly, slowly, the pieces were falling into place.

Two weeks ago, more or less, Reva Adams had been assigned to research a mysterious project at this base.

Shortly thereafter, the transmitter at her building had gone into action.

Immediately, the thinking of the entire body of personnel had grown distorted—as witness MacDougal's order to build an apparently useless tower in the face of The Project's alleged failure.

Then he, Carl Stone, had returned—and the transmitter hadn't affected him, save to make him abnormally tense and irritable and nervous.

Reva had diagnosed him as an encephalitis victim.

And now, in Quinn, he'd discovered another encephalitic—and apparently Quinn's thinking hadn't been distorted by the transmitter, either! He'd retained his judgment, his ability to analyze and reason, in spite of admitted irritability and tension.

In other words, whatever else the transmitter might have done, it hadn't been able to influence encephalitic intellects.

Why?

Staring at his cup, Stone pondered.

"There's tissue damage," Reva had said, *"and, later, of course, residual lesions. Ganglion cells and neurons degenerate or disappear."*

That meant that the functioning of the brain was changed, impaired.

The transmitter at Reva's project building pulsed out waves that distorted the thinking of normal brains.

But encephalitics didn't have normal brains. The disease destroyed cells, burned out synapses.

So, in them, the transmitter merely heightened tension. Scar tissue slashed gaps its impulses couldn't bridge.

OF A sudden Stone felt better than he had in days. This discovery—it was a step forward; a long, long step.

The only trouble was, he still had so far to go.

For instance, where did the monsters fit into the picture?

The robots?

How did they link to the transmitter?

And—the thought came in spite of all his efforts to shut it out—to Reva?

Because there *was* a link. There had to be. The problem was only to establish the chain of logic.

He took another sip of coffee; spoke as much to himself as to his companions: "First, I smashed the transmitter. Then, the monsters came—"

"The monsters—?" The thin-faced Dawes hunched forward eagerly, seeming glad for the sudden change of subject. "I haven't heard anything about a transmitter. But these monsters—now there's something I can get my teeth in!"

"You can have 'em," Quinn grunted sourly. "Me, I wouldn't get my teeth in a monster if I was starving."

"No kidding, Quinn! I just wish I'd have seen one!" Dawes' brown eyes sparkled. "They're aliens, obviously—extraterrestrials from some other planet. Also, they've mastered space travel—which means they're superior to humans, no matter what they look like. Look how they handled the business with the robots—kidnapping our base director as a hostage, along with a psychiatrist to give 'em a hand at figuring out our mental mechanisms. Personally, I don't think there'd have been any trouble with them whatever, if people hadn't panicked. But when those women out in the prefabs saw 'em—all tentacles and whatnot—everybody stopped thinking. The troops didn't do any good, either. The aliens didn't have any choice but to fight back, once the lead started flyng . . ."

The monsters. The tentacles.

The dead woman. Glines. Bjornberg.

Without avail, Stone tried to black out the picture. In spite of himself, he shuddered.

He knew, then, that for him there could never be any compromise with the strange creatures. No matter what he should learn, regardless of any answers the future might uncover, he could never hope to throw off his horror. His memories were too black, too bitter.

Dawes was still talking: ". . . and I wonder how many of us have ever stopped to consider the functional aspects of multiple tentacles. Just think how handy it'd be to have suction cups on the ends of your fingers! It's as great an evolutionary development as the thumb! And there's the business of having the tentacles on both ends of the body, too—your feet get tired, so you turn upside down and walk on the other end. The stripe around the middle is probably a sensor band—a continuous nerve unit that sees, hears, tastes, smells; that is, assuming they have our senses. Or maybe they ingest their food from the air, by osmosis, the way a frog does water—"

The flow of words showed no signs of stopping. All at once, Stone could take no more. He had to be alone, to think.

Abruptly, he rose. "Quinn—Dawes—I want to thank you both," he interrupted. "You've been a big help—more than you know."

He started to turn.

As he did so, the blaring radio down by the other occupied table went into a sudden, crackling spasm, then fell silent.

A coffee-drinker rose, reached for the dials.

But before he could touch them, the radio blared again. A voice spoke—a strange, metallic voice like none that Stone had ever heard:

"Base! Development base called Las Crescentes! I speaking to you!"

Stone went rigid. Chairs scraped at the other table.

"Listen, Base! I speaking!"

THE man who had risen from the far table twisted the volume dial.

"Listen, Base! Listen, Base! Listen, Base . . ." The level of the strange voice stayed constant.

The man moved the selector.

The voice came in on all bands.

The man stumbled back, white-faced and shaking. An icy finger ran up and down Stone's spine.

The clanging, harsh, metallic voice went on:

"Listen, Base! I here at World Earth from world you not know. I get element you call krypton. Must have. Take out you air. Not hurt."

Stone groped. "Krypton—?"

Quinn speaking: "Inert gas, one part in six or seven hundred thousand in normal atmosphere."

The voice again: "Must have! Take! You help, I not hurt."

"Aliens!" Dawes' nails scraped the table. "I was right! I was right!"

The voice: "Tower take. You run. Must have!"

"'Tower take'?" Quinn's eyes narrowed. "My God! You don't suppose—"

"Listen, Base—!"

A pause. Then, a new voice on the speaker, deep and familiar.

MacDougal's voice; thick with tension.

"John MacDougal speaking."

Stone gripped the back of his chair so hard his knuckles ached.

MacDougal: "As you've probably guessed, our visitors tonight are from—elsewhere. Another planet. Maybe even another solar system. I'm not quite sure. There's a problem in communication. They don't have anything like what we'd term normal speech apparatus. They'd tried to get around it with the mechanical substitute you just heard, but it's pretty limited."

A pause, vibrant with nerve-shattering silence.

"Anyhow, they want krypton. Why, I don't know. They just keep saying 'Must have!'"

Another pause, longer this time.

Stone's muscles were knotting.

"This krypton—we're to get it for them." MacDougal sounded old and frightened now. "They've even equipped us to do the job. It seems they've—been around quite a while. A couple of weeks, anyhow. So they did a little mind con-

trol work on one of our people, Doctor Reva Adams. Again, I don't quite know how; probably they're telepaths—maybe that's how they communicate with each other. In any case, they maneuvered things so she set up a transmitter that induced what amounted to a mild paranoia in all base personnel." A short laugh, more panic than mirth. "Including me, the base director . . ."

With an effort, Stone twisted the chair about and sat down. Within him, the tension kept climbing. If it went on—wildly, he wondered if a man could feel his own sanity slipping away . . .

MacDougal again, sounding more like himself this time: "Sorry, friends. I'm all right, and so is Doctor Adams. Just chalk up any breaks I make to nerves . . ." He spoke less jerkily now. His voice came through the radio's amplifier strong and steady.

STONE'S tension ebbed a fraction. He leaned forward, concentrating on the base director's every word:

". . . I spoke of paranoia. As you may know, the disorder's marked by systematized delusions and hallucinations. In my own case, these centered on a conviction that I'd developed a new and revolutionary approach to The Project. Backing it up, I ordered construction of the equipment that now occupies the tower on top of the Central Project Building. In turn, the rest of you fell into a pattern that blocked off any questioning of my judgment, and built up resistance—extreme hostilty, in fact—to any thought or suggestion that might threaten the work or the aliens.

"Actually, of course, my 'new development' had nothing whatever to do with The Project. On the contrary. The only function the device has is to extract krypton from the atmosphere as fast and efficiently as possible. How it works, I can't say; the design's so different from anything we know that I'm inclined to think it's based on scientific principles completely outside our experience.

"Some of you may wonder why these aliens picked our base as a place to set up their operation. Apparently there were two reasons: First, The Project involved materials and a good deal of hard-to-fabricate equipment that they needed for their krypton extraction process. Second, Las Crescentes is isolated. Their mind-control transmitter blanketed us without overlapping into any other inhabited areas, so they didn't have to worry about outside interference.

"That brings up another point: These creatures have a wave-shielding device that tops anything we know. That's how they cut in on your radios with this broadcast. It also blocks off your transmitters and telephone equipment, so don't waste time trying to get outside help.

"Getting back to the other aspects of the situation, this is the way it stacks up: If everything had gone according to plan, we'd have finished the extraction unit in the tower, drained Earth's atmosphere of krypton, and delivered it to these aliens. Probably we wouldn t even have realized what we'd done till after they'd left the planet.

"Fortunately or unfortunately, though, something went wrong. One of our base security men, Carl Stone, was in Washington when these creatures moved in. Last night he got back. For some reason neither the aliens nor I can quite figure out, the paranoia transmitter didn't affect him. He recognized that something was wrong on the base, and he wouldn't be pressured into letting it slide. In less time than seems possible, he located the transmitter and smashed it.

"The moment the transmitter went off, the aliens knew something was wrong. They moved in on the base.

"Our troops stopped that, fast. The aliens saw they'd have to fight a pitched battle to take over. They drew back instead. Maybe they're humanitarians. Or maybe they were afraid the tower might be wrecked if shooting started. I don't know.

"Anyhow, they sent the flying robots for Doctor Adams and me. We're hostage-interpreters, I gather.

"That brings up the reason I'm talking. I'm supposed to tell you what they want you to do.

"It's simple enough: Just finish the krypton extractor according to plan just as fast as possible—they figure twenty-four hours ought to do the job.

"Then, put it into operation. They'll supply cylinders to store the krypton.

"Once it's aboard their ship, they'll turn Doctor Adams and me loose and be on their way to wherever they're going.

"They want me to hit it hard that this won't cost us anything. To us, krypton's just an inert gas, with no practical value. To them, for some reason, it's vital. They say they'll even pay us off for it by giving us whatever scraps of scientific information they've got that we're capable of absorbing.

"On the other hand—"—now MacDougal's voice developed the faintest of tremors—"—if we don't go along a hundred per cent, they promise immediate, utter and com-plete destruction of the base, and extermination of all personnel—after which, they'll pick another site for their plant and try again."

The base director paused, then; hesitated, fumbled while the silence echoed.

In the snack bar, tension climbed and eddied like a thermal updraft. Stone could hear the harsh rasp of his companions' breathing.

For his own part, he dared not even suck in air, for fear his self-control would crack.

"I guess that's all," MacDougal said at last. Again, as at the beginning, his voice suddenly sounded old and frightened. "I'm in no position to try to influence your decision. I don't have the right to tell you what to do, or how to do it. Make up your own minds and—and good luck—"

He broke off. Once more, the silence echoed.

Then, like a thunder-clap, the alien's clanging, metallic voice cut in—harsh, savage: "Listen, Base! I speaking! Get krypton! Must have!

"Get krypton—or die!"

The radio went dead . . .

CHAPTER VII

FEAR stalked the base. It hung in the air . . . seeped through the hush . . . showed in trembling hands and on strained faces.

Stone felt it, too. Fear and something else.

Something that crawled and gnawed and ached within him. Something that reached out spidery tendrils to the farthest cell of his very being.

It came out in a name, pulsing in his brain: Reva . . . Reva . . . Reva . . .

He paced the night, hour after hour. But nowhere, nohow, could he escape her. Misty and wraith-like, her face swayed before him. The soft curve of her cheek, the scent of her hair, the taste of her lips—they wouldn't leave him alone.

Her eyes were the worst: Gentle grey eyes, imploring . . .

He cursed aloud in the stillness.

Only there was nothing he could do. Nothing.

Seething, he sought out the headquarters.

A young captain looked up as he entered.

Stone said, "Well? What's the decision?"

"Decision?" The officer shrugged. "We're till waiting. That tank unit's coming. We got through to it before the bugs clamped down their wave-shield."

"But Doctor Adams—MacDougal—"

"The base comes first. We can't risk it—not just for two prisoners."

Stone choked harsh words off unspoken. Pivoting, he strode back out into the darkness.

A whole base, versus two prisoners.

Calculated risk, and the greatest good of the greatest number.

The commandant's attitude made sense. Of course it did.

Except for one thing:

One of the prisoners was Reva.

Only that was individual, personal, a pain deep inside him. The commandant didn't know about that. And even if he did, he couldn't afford to let it matter.

The answer? Stone scuffed at the gravel. That was the trouble: There just wasn't any answer.

Or was there?

Suppose you reversed the equation, turned the figures upside down.

The commandant saw two lives against thousands. That was his duty.

But for him, Carl Stone, it was different. He had one life; that was all.

One life, to gamble for two. His own neck to risk, on the off chance that he might save MacDougal and Reva.

It was a good thought. It made the odds look different.

Stone laughed abruptly. Who was

he kidding? The odds didn't matter, nor even MacDougal. Reva was the one who counted, and Reva only.

Because he loved her. In spite of everything, he loved her.

It was decision.

Stone's breathing quickened. All at once he felt alive again, no longer numb or bowed down. The years, the bitterness, the heartbreak—like shackles struck off, as one they fell away. Cool, purposeful, his stride firm, he struck out towards the Central Project Area's main gate.

The weary guards waved him by on the strength of his security pass. Beyond the last barrier, then, he broke into a dogtrot and stayed with it all the way to the administration building lot where his car was parked.

One brief detour, to his quarters to pick up a thirty-eight. Then out onto the highway, heading east towards the spot where he'd watched the woman die.

The sky was greying now, along the horizon far ahead; another day aborning, out of the chill shadows of a desert dawn.

Bleakly, Stone wondered if he'd live to see it end.

Then tire-churned gravel marked the turn-off point. Slowing to low gear, Stone wrenched the steering wheel around and bumped off the road, out across the shoulder into the open desert.

THE trail the woman had left proved surprisingly easy to follow, still—a broken creosote bush here, kicked-over clumps of fishhook cactus there, ground shoe-scraped in between.

The tracks pointed to a high, rocky tableland perhaps three miles back from the road.

What was it the dying woman had said—"robots beyond the mesa"—?

The back of Stone's neck prickled.

His car gave out less than three-quarters of a mile from the road, ambushed by rocks and a mesquite tree.

Stolidly, Stone abandoned it and set out on foot. The trail, at first so clear, had vanished now, so he set his course for the mesa and hoped for the best.

Slowly, the sun edged up. The day began to warm.

Stone plodded on, dodging cactus and keeping a sharp eye out for snakes.

He was nearly to the hill when he heard the helicopter. Before he could find a place to hide, it was hovering directly overhead . . . settling slowly, rotor whishing.

Hastily, Stone slid his gun out of sight beneath his coat and stood waiting.

Landing on a nearby patch of open ground, the whirlybird's pilot threw open the door. "Hey, you!"

"Yes?" Stone picked his way toward the craft. "What is it?"

The pilot scowled. "You're out of bounds. I got orders to come out and pick you up. The CO's taking no chances of getting those bugs stirred up till he knows just where we stand."

"I might have known that gateguard would say something about me." Stone managed a rueful smile. "Well, so goes it . . ."

He clambered into the helicopter. not even protesting; closed the door. The pilot manipulated the controls. The engine roared. Slowly, the 'copter rose, straight up into the air.

Stone reached beneath his coat. Not even bothering to speak, he brought out the thirty-eight and leveled it at the other's side.

"Hey!" The pilot stiffened. "Put that thing away. You want to get into trouble?"

"I'm already in it, friend," Stone said gently. "I might as well go whole hog." He gestured with the revolver's muzzle. "Let's have a look on the other side of that mesa."

Muttering, the pilot sent the helicopter higher.

Only then, before they had more than reached the edge of the tableland, a sound bore in upon them . . . a high, shrill, droning sound . . .

It was Stone's turn to stiffen. Swiveling in his seat, he peered out, searching.

Beyond the mesa, a flight of the flying robots climbed into view in a swift, tight spiral, swirling up and around straight into the morning sun.

Simultaneously, the pilot exclaimed, "Look—! The tanks!"

Stone strained his eyes.

Far off in the eastern desert, tiny beetle-like vehicles ground slowly towards them, churning up long streamers of dust. A distant sound of firing, heavy guns, echoed on the morning breeze.

In the same instant, the first of the tanks lurched from its path. The distance was too great for Stone to tell just what had happened. He only knew that the armored titan was veering, jerking, rolling over.

A fraction of a second later it dissappeared in a spurting, concussive burst of flame.

Now beyond it, a second vehicle was in trouble. A third.

The fourth exploded like a gigantic exclamation point of fire.

From then on, the battle turned into a rout.

With no survivors.

Sickness twisted at Stone's belly. Fighting it down, he swung back to the pilot. "I won't risk your neck, lieutenant. Land me on the mesa, and be on your way."

WORDLESS, the pilot shifted the whirlybird's controls, setting the 'copter down on a rocky plateau.

"If your CO bawls you out, remind him I had a gun," Stone said. He opened the door; jumped to the ground.

The helicopter was rising again almost before he could turn.

But not for long.

Because suddenly, seemingly out of nowhere, half-a-dozen flying robots swooped down.

Stone never could be sure that the pilot even saw them. They came that fast.

As they passed over the 'copter, the one in the lead dipped slightly. A tentacle speared out, whipped round; stabbed into the blur of spinning rotor blades.

Then it caught, with a jerk so violent that the robot spun from its course, too fast for the eye to follow.

But only for a moment. Then, bobber-like, it came into balance again, the rotor still dangling from the tentacle.

Like a crippled bird, the helicopter plunged earthward . . .

struck with a rending crash . . . shattered into flames.

Shuddering, Stone crouched motionless in the shadow of a boulder.

Yet, incredibly, the robots gave no sign that they sensed his presence. A moment later they were gone.

Tight-lipped, Stone left his haven and trudged on across the mesa. A mile. Two.

Then, abruptly, the tableland fell away before him. Dropping flat on his belly by the rim, he stared down in grim fascination into the canyon below; for there, surely, lay one of the strangest things the eyes of man had ever seen.

It was a sphere—a shining gigantic metal ball, fully three hundred feet in diameter, if Stone could judge. No lines or ports or crevices marred its gleaming surface. Nowhere about it could he see any sign of life.

Quickly he drew back from the rim, well out of view of the sphere. Then, rising, he strode left, following the mesa's edge till he came to a spot where the eroded lip cut back enough to hide him from the globe-shaped craft.

Slipping and falling, bruising and tearing, he descended to the canyon's floor, then made his way back towards the sphere.

Here, studying it at a lower level from a hidden vantage-point amid the talus, he gained a better, clearer picture.

Three stubby legs gave the globe balance on the uneven bedrock of the canyon floor. A broad, inclined ramp led to a slot-like belly hatch. Of mosters or robots he could see no trace.

Stone sucked in air—a long, deep breath. This was the thing he'd sought, the aliens' ship; and now he'd found it.

To what avail?

Somewhere in its maw, by all odds, lay Reva and MacDougal. Yet what could he do about it? How could he, alone and armed only with his Smith & Wesson, hope to invade it or to save them?

But he'd known the odds before he started—and he'd still come. Logic and hazard simply had no bearing.

Surging up, gun in hand, he moved warily forward, hugging the mesa wall.

Now he came abreast the sphere. The ramp to the belly hatch beckoned, smooth and inviting.

Inviting as madness.

A nervous spasm knotted Stone's belly. When it had passed, he stepped out from the wall moved forward, cat-footed, towards the ramp.

Still nothing happened.

Going around the edge of the ramp, he peered up through the open hatch, into the sphere-ship.

THE interior shone with a dim, greenish glow. Overhead loomed a bulwark. He could see nothing more. The stillness was deafening, unbroken save by the whisper of the desert breeze far above.

A new chill shook him.

He might have turned back, then. He almost did.

But in that same moment, as he started to draw away, a voice echoed thinly deep in the globe-craft.

Reva's voice, ragged and strainstraught.

It caught Stone like a magnet. His doubts fell forgotten. Soundlessly, he swung up onto the ramp... crept shadow-silent on into the hatchway.

A corridor yawned, dim in the ghostly green glow. Hardly daring to breathe, Stone sidled along it past doors, littered chambers.

It ended at a tube-like, vertical shaft set off by a guard-rail.

The ship's axis, probably.

Stone strained his ears, listening. Again Reva's voice came—louder, this time; vibrating down the shaft.

Swinging out over the guard-rail, Stone peered upward.

The shaft was smooth as glass—without hand-holds or bracing.

He dropped back to the corridor floor.

A closed double door to his left,

next to the shaft, tempted him. He stepped towards it.

Like magic, it parted before him, silent as death. A steep ramp curved to the right, following the tube-shaft.

Finger tense on the thrty-eight's trigger, he moved up it, higher and higher.

Each ninety degrees arced brought a new door, a new level. When he approached them, they opened; when they opened he listened.

And each time, Reva's voice sounded closer.

He could hear MacDougal, too, now, on occasion, speaking in rumbles. The very nearness brought sweat oozing. A dozen times he had to switch the gun from one hand to the other to scrub his palms dry of slickness.

Another level. Another. Another. *The* level.

Tension drew a band tight over his chest—compressing, constricting. His neck ached. His blood pounded.

Jaws tight, gun-hand rigid, he moved down the passage.

A doorway. An open doorway, flooding out brighter, whiter light.

Back to the wall, Stone edged to it . . . stared into the room it revealed.

Reva sat on a low, curving divan across from MacDougal. Her pale face showed deep strain-lines; her hands twisted, white-knuckled.

MacDougal's whole body sagged limp and exhausted. The shaggy brows stood out over eyes deep-sunk in dark hollows. His right arm hung in a sling.

Stone swayed for a moment, not daring to think, then slid forward —taut, noiseless.

MacDougal's head twitched. His eyes flicked towards the doorway.

"Quiet—!" Stone shook as he whispered. "For God's sake, be quiet!"

Reva, MacDougal—they both jerked like puppets.

Stone hissed, "This way—quick!"

MacDougal's jowls quivered. His left hand gripped the divan as he heaved up from it.

Eyes distended, breasts rising and falling too fast, Reva followed.

Stone stepped back.

The tentacles folded round him, then.

He triggered his gun by sheer reflex.

The thirty-eight roared—wild, aimless. The bullet rang, bouncing off metal.

The tentacles only drew relentlessly tighter. One slapped at the gun, tore it loose from his fingers.

Another looped round his throat.

It was like a nightmare—a mad repetition of that blood-curdling moment outside Reva's building.

The tentacle drew tighter. Stone's lungs exploded.

The blackness closed in . . .

CHAPTER VIII

THE man beside Stone kept talking, talking:

"They let you get all the way in before they grabbed you, didn't they? They like it like that—to lead you on, coax you, let you think you're going to win before they kill you. That's how they played it with me. And my wife. Did I tell you about her? They let her run and run, clear across the mesa. All the way down to the highway. Only then a car stopped, so they grabbed her and killed her. They told me about it. They thought it was the best joke ever . . ."

Stone tried to sit up, to focus on the speaker.

He fell instead, retching.

The man said, "Don't worry. You're not really hurt. It's just those damn tentacles, those snake-things they use for arms. They choke you, and tear you, and scare you so you get sick just thinking about 'em. I know. I had it, that night on the mesa—"

"Y o u—"—Stone half-choked—"—you . . . saw robots?"

"Robots—?" A quavering laugh. "Sure, I saw robots. Robots on the mesa. That's how it all started. Ellen and I—we didn't know it was a government reservation. We were out for some fun. Some fun! Prospecting, believe it or not—prospecting for uranium with a home-made Geiger. Just a fool high-school science teacher and his wife, out on vacation. Only then we got up on the mesa, and I saw the robots. Ellen was scared, but I said, Let's get closer. So they saw us—the squids, here. Caught me. Killed Ellen. Poor Ellen. . ."

The man's shoulders shook. Then jerked, harder and harder. Anguished sounds came from his throat in dry, racking spasms. "Poor Ellen —"

Stone fought his own stomach; won, lurched up, still panting. Slowly, his vision cleared.

Beside him, the stranger sobbed more wildly. He no longer seemed even aware of Stone's presence. "Why'd they have to leave me, Ellen? Why didn't they kill me, too? That's what I wanted. But no, they had to have someone to go out in the sun. They can't stand the sun, can they, Ellen? Oh—Ellen—!"

His voice rose to a shriek. His face came up into the light—cheeks and chin stubble-matted, eyes wild and staring.

With an effort, Stone reached out and caught one jerking shoulder. Savagely, he slapped the man's face, palm and backhand.

The racking sobs slowed. Wonderingly, the man slumped to the floor, rubbing his cheek. "You—you hit me . . ." No anger rang in his words—only baffled incredulity, the puzzlement of a hurt child. His eyes stayed wide open, appallingly empty.

Pain under his breastbone, Stone said, "Sorry, friend. You were going to pieces. You've got to get steady or you won't last long, here or elsewhere."

"Last long? Last long?" The other fondled the words. "Who's going to last long, once the squids get their krypton?" A wild giggle. "You know about krypton? Did they tell you?"

Stone felt himself stiffen. "What about krypton?"

"'Must have!'" Again, the man giggled. "Can't run a spaceship without any krypton. Can't fly the robots. Can't even blast a little ole Earth city. 'Krypton! Must have!' They'll get it, too. From that base. It's already surrendered. The people were scared, just like we are. Especially after what happened to the tanks. So the whole base surrendered and started working on that extractor, the krypton extractor. They'll have it finished by tomorrow morning. Then the squids'll get their krypton. And they'll keep their promise

too—not hurt anybody, leave right after they get it. They all say so. That'll be the best joke of all—a whole world doing a pratfall right into hell. The squids'll laugh and laugh and laugh, all the way back to Arcturus Four, or Betelgeuse, or wherever it is they come from. Except they can't go back. Not really. They're outlaws, you know, running away from their own species. That's how they happened to get this far from their source of krypton. 'Krypton! Must have!' Can't run a space ship without that vital krypton—"

THE stiffness in Stone had turned to sudden chill. He caught the babbling man's shirtfront; shook him roughly. "Run that through again, . . . the part about the joke, the world doing a prat-fall!"

A vacuous smile. "You really don't know? You don't know about krypton? I thought only fool high-school science teachers didn't know. And Ellen. Poor Ellen—"

"The krypton! What about the krypton?"

"It's a gas, that's all. An inert gas. About two parts to a million of air. It's not worth anything. Nobody wants krypton. Nobody but the squids. Who cares about a little ole catalyst?"

"A catalyst—?"

"Sure. Doesn't do anything it-self; just changes the rate of a reaction. Try to light dry phos-phorus, what happens? Nothing. Dampen the air a little, it burns like a house afire. Water's the catalyst. Atmosphere's the same way. Mix oxygen and nitrogen and everything else but krypton—it just dissipates, leaks away into space. Shoot in two parts of kry-pton to a million, it holds toge-ther like a sack around ole Mother Earth. That's why there's no breathable atmosphere on so many planets. No krypton. Do we know that? No. But the squids know it. That's why they're laughing. Why should they waste time blasting us? Soon's they get our krypton, our atmosphere thins away—*poof!* like that— and we all drop dead. The squids don't care; they don't breathe air like we do. It's the best joke they've had since they blew up Vega Seven . . ."

Stone's legs were suddenly too weak to hold him. His compan-ion's continuing compulsive word-flood echoed unheeded.

The whole world doing a prat-fall into hell.

Stone's flesh crawled. The poor, **tortured** creature beside him had **phrased** it too well. It turned a

man's mind off, froze his brain . . . left him clutching in free fall with-out strength even to shudder.

Yet there was nothing he could do—nothing, nothing. Not here, sealed in this green-glowing, metal walled room with a madman for company.

A madman—? There'd be two of them soon. Two lunatics, giggling and babbling as the atmosphere thinned and they slowly strangled.

Or would you strangle? Maybe, with the pressure change, your lungs would burst first . . .

Stone surged to his feet in a spasm of frenzy. Savagely, he hurled himself at the door—beat-ing it, tearing at the crack with his fingers till the nails broke and blood streamed, weird in the green glow.

His companion stared at him, wide-eyed. "You're hurting your hands. Is something the matter?"

"The matter—?" Stone shook with fury, frustration. "No, noth-ing's the matter. The base has surrendered. The monsters get our krypton. Our air leaks away. The whole planet dies. Every-thing's fine—fine . . ."

He broke off, unable to go on.

"Oh . . ." The other sounded hurt, plaintive. Then: "Well, why don't you stop it? Call the base. Have them blow up the extractor."

"Call — the — base — ?"   Stone

stopped breathing.

"Yes. The machine's in a room right down the hall, here."

Stone choked back his tension . . . spoke gently, soothingly: "Our door's locked.

"Oh, that." His companion giggled. "Leave that to me. I'll get us out of here."

Already, he was scrambling to his feet; stripping off his shirt.

"But if you can get out . . ." Stone groped.

"It takes two." Tearing the ragged shirt into broad strips, the man hummed a fragment of tune. "I thought it all out. If I'd had Ellen with me— I can run the machine, too. I watched them do it. It's very clever. Sets up a force field, distorts radio waves. Using energy derived from krypton, of course. Always krypton. 'Must have!'" He broke off. "I'll need your shirt, too, please. And your jacket. Got to have cloth. Lots of cloth . . ."

Wordless, Stone turned over his garments.

DEFTLY, the man ripped them into more of the broad strips . . . tied the strips together in a long, rope-like band perhaps six inches wide. He'd stopped talking now. An occasional mirthless chuckle replaced his giggling.

The job done, he handed Stone one end of the strip. "Now stand here, please. Right beside the door. That's all you need to do. Just stand there, and hold onto the cloth. I'll take care of everything else. Just you wait and see . . ."

He kicked off a shoe; hammered the edge of the sole on the door.

It made a dull, clanging noise. "They don't like this. It'll get our door open. Just you wait—"

Stone waited—sweating, staring numbly.

It was a fine way to end up— playing games with a madman.

Only he had no choice.

The next instant, the door burst open. Tentacles vibrating furiously, one of the aliens swept into the room.

The man with Stone stepped back lithely, dodging the creature. The wide, vacant eyes shone bright, now; teeth showed clenched behind the empty smile.

The alien surged towards him.

Again, the man leaped back, the cloth strip coiled loose between his hands.

The alien reached for him.

But instead of retreating, the man darted in close. Deftly, as a matador swirling his cape past a charging bull, he slapped the cloth strip over the monster's scarlet sensor band.

The rope snapped tight in Stone's hands as the alien lurched against it, then tried to draw back.

But the man would not let it. Racing round it, he whipped the fabric strip tight into place, completely covering the creature's narrow scarlet girdle.

Heedless of tentacles, Stone leaped to join him.

The cloth reached three times around the monster's midriff. The alien reeled blindly—groping, uncertain. Its tentacles' movements seemed mostly directed at tearing free the fabric. When a disc caught Stone's shoulder, he jerked it loose with no skin loss.

"Come on!" This from the madman. "Quick! This way! Hurry!"

Stumbling through the doorway, Stone sprinted down the corridor after him.

Now another door loomed, close by the tube-shaft. "Here!"

Stone threw himself at it.

It burst open under his impact. He crashed to the floor of the chamber beyond, barely glimpsing a mass of equipment as he fell.

Equipment—and another alien.

The thing flung itself on Stone, its tentacles twining.

Savagely, he twisted; drove his heels up with all his strength, straight at the monster's sensor band.

The alien rocked back.

Stone leaped up. Then, head low, he charged in, smashing the monster back into the doorway by sheer bull strength and violence.

Another charge—butting; fists slamming.

The alien hit the guard-rail encircling the tube-shaft.

Stone glimpsed blurring motion: His fellow-prisoner, diving in low and bear-hugging tentacles. Through his red haze of fury, it came to Stone dimly that the other's last shred of sanity must have departed.

Only then, of a sudden, the man was surging up, jerking.

The knee-leverage tore the alien's lower tentacles loose from the floor. With a heave, the man flipped the creature over the rail.

It plummeted down the tube-shaft.

"Two hundred feet!" Stone's companion cried shrilly. "Listen! It may spatter—!"

NAUSEA writhed in Stone. He caught the other about the waist; dragged him bodily back into the room—up to the equipment.

"Quick! How do I work this?"

"Don't worry. It's easy." The man tugged at a smooth, round shaft of metal. A faint humming sound rose from a flat gridwork.

"There. It's on now. Just talk into the grill, there."

Stone had trouble with breathing: "Base! Las Crescentes—"

Behind him, metal rang on metal. He spun round.

An alien stood poised in the doorway—an alien with shreds of cloth still clinging round its middle.

The words he'd planned stuck in his throat.

Only then, as from afar, another voice echoed. The voice of the madman.

"You know—"—it was almost conversational, the way he said it—"—you know, I think I'll go see Ellen . . ."

He scooped a jagged strip of metal from a bench as he spoke. Traces of froth showed at the corners of his mouth.

Then, before Stone could move, he was lunging, straight at the monster. The metal strip slashed deep into the scarlet sensor band. Fluid spurted.

The alien hurled itself backward.

But like one possessed, the madman pursued it, hacking and gouging. Together, man and monster crashed into the guard-rail.

A wild shriek of mad laughter. "Here I come, Ellen—with company!"

Clutching a dozen tentacles, the man hurled himself over the guard-rail.

The monster went with him.

Stone clung to the transmitter, half-retching.

Only he couldn't afford to be sick. Not here; not now.

Time was too short for that. Any moment now, there'd be other aliens coming.

Hoarsely, he rasped, "Base! Las Crescentes! This is Carl Stone talking. I'm giving you an order: Destroy that tower! Blast it! Don't wait a minute! If it goes into operation, the whole earth will die . . ."

CHAPTER IX

TOGETHER, they stood at last in the free air of the desert—Stone, Reva, MacDougal.

Slowly, half a mile away, the great shining metal ball that was the alien sphere-ship lifted from the gathering shadows of the canyon floor. Soundless as nightfall it rose, drifting higher and higher. The three stub legs retracted.

Then, of a sudden, it had topped the mesa's rim. Faster it climbed, and faster, picking up speed with every passing second.

The blink of an eye later it was gone, up into the dusk and the boundless space that stretched from star to star.

For a long, long moment the silence held. Then MacDougal said quietly, "There aren't any words for what I want to say, Carl. But —the world can never repay you for what you've done."

And Reva:"You saved us. Carl —us, and all the unborn generations that will ever live on Earth."

It was strange, Stone thought. By all the rules, he should feel the same way they did. Happy, Relieved. At peace.

Grateful for the breaks he'd gotten, at least.

Instead, inside, he felt only aching emptiness and pain.

But however he felt, he had to find words. They were expected. The other—the ugly, unfinished job he had yet to do—that could wait.

Shrugging, he said, "The boys at the base are the ones who rate the credit. They worked fast—two minutes flat from the time I passed the word till they shot an anti-tank grenade right into the middle of that damn' tower, if our friends the monsters had it right."

"You're over-modest, Carl." MacDougal gestured with his still sling-bound right arm. "You're the one who did the job, and I'm going to see that people know it. The right people."

"Thanks." The word came out faintly caustic, even to Stone's ears.

But maybe that was only the aftermath of strain.

If MacDougal caught it, he ignored it. His craggy face stayed tolerant, relaxed. The hedgerow eyebrows didn't even bristle.

"The big point is, it's over," he reminded. "The aliens and their ship are gone. Our own world's safe."

Reva moved restlessly, drawing her torn dress closer about her, as if touched by a sudden chill. "I hope so. I still don't feel quite as if I were awake. There's so much I don't understand—so many, many things. . ."

Stone's voice was just above a whisper: "For instance—?"

"You mean—you haven't thought about it? —About why those creatures' didn't harm the base, in spite of all their threats? Why they let us go, when it would have been so much easier to kill us?"

Stone didn't answer.

MacDougal said, "I think it's easy enough to understand. The aliens' whole technology is based on krypton, and it's in short supply. Destroying the base would have cut down what little reserve they had left, with no return."

"And letting us go—?"

The base director's **heavy**

shoulders shifted. "That's almost a rhretorical question, isn't it, Doctor Adams?" The slightest of edges barbed his words.

Deep in Stone's middle, the pain and emptiness seethed anew.

That was the trouble with unfinished jobs. They kept forcing themselves onto you, when you least wanted to have to think about them.

Only now this particular ugliness was coming out into the open in spite of him. He'd have to face it, grapple with it.

Even if it tore his soul apart.

R EVA was staring at Mac-Dougal. "Rhetorical—? I don't understand. What do you mean?"

"Then I'm afraid I'll have to be brutal, Doctor." The base director let out a gusty, sighing breath. "Perhaps you don't realize the nasty role you've played in this whole business. If so, I'm sorry. But the fact remains that in all likelihood Stone and I are alive and free only because of you."

His tone made Reva draw back just a little. Once more, she pulled her torn dress about her, with a movement strangely awkward for one so graceful.

"You'll have to speak more plainly, Mr. MacDougal," she said sharply. "I don't understand you at all."

"Very well, then." MacDougal's massive head came forward, jaw belligerently outthrust. "I'm saying flat-out that you were the aliens' contact. Your mind was the one they took over when they first landed. You were the one who set up the transmitter in your project building and turned the whole base mad. Is that plain enough for you to understand?"

The torn dress bunched under Reva's fingers, an ugly, lumpy wad.

MacDougal again: "I'll carry it even further, Doctor. The aliens don't plan to drop that contact with you. And that's the only reason why the three of us are free."

Even through the gathering dusk, Stone could see the pallor that sprang to Reva's face. Fear widened her eyes. She seemed to grow smaller, older.

It twisted like a knife inside him . . . made him wonder bleakly how long he could go on.

"Did you think they'd really left for good, Doctor Adams?" The base director's sarcasm rang open, bitter, now. "How far do you estimate they can go—with their krypton reserves already so drained that they didn't even dare to blast our base? To Aldebaran? Antares? Alpha Centauri?" He laughed—curt, scornful. "No, Doctor! They'll be back, somewhere close by, in hours, not lightyears.

Then, when they get here, they'll contact you. There'll be another transmitter, another base gone mad. And this time, maybe, they'll get their krypton—that is, if Stone and I are fools enough to let you live!"

There it was, out in the open. All of it.

Or almost all.

The blood rang in Stone's ears.

Reva's face was a twisted, distorted thing. Her face seemed to crack. Her lips peeled back. "No, no!" She was half-screaming. "You're wrong! You're wrong—!"

The base director swung his thick, sling-bound right arm—hammering, relentless. "Then why did they let us live? Why—except to keep you free and above suspicion, ready to serve them another day?"

Silence. Echoing eternities of silence.

Then, abruptly, Reva's shoulders slumped. Her chin sank to her chest. She didn't speak.

Slowly, MacDougal straightened. Grim-faced, he looked at Stone. "Well, Carl?"

More silence. A sickness, too . . . gnawing through Stone, body and brain.

Why dd it have to be like this? Why couldn't it have ended another way?

MacDougal said, "I'm sorry, Carl. I know how you feel. But this is just too big for us. We can't take chances. The world's at stake. We've got to act now, before the aliens come back."

Stone couldn't speak.

"She can't be allowed to leave this spot alive, Carl. You and I— we'll have to serve as judge and jury. Executioners too. Here. Now."

Stone looked at Reva.

Her eyes were upon him. Grey eyes, imploring. "Carl—!"

MacDougal: "I'm sorry, Carl . . ."

Tension. Surging billows of tenion. Blood pulsing. Heart pounding. *Why couldn't it have ended another way?*

Only this was the way it was. These were the cards he had to play.

So he'd play them—

Stone said, "You've figured it right, Mac. All but one point.

"One—? What—?"

"She isn't guilty. You are."

T HE base director stood like a graven image. Then his sling hand twitched, just a fraction. That was all.

Stone said, "It all rides on one thing, Mac: You keep talking about the aliens having some sort of mind control over Reva. But it's not true. Violence is the only weapon they know how to use."

MacDougal's lip twisted. "You

forget the transmitter."

"The transmitter?" Stone shook his head slowly. "That came second, Mac. Not first. Because somebody had to help the aliens design it—somebody working of his own free will."

"She did it, then. She's the psychiatrist."

"No, Mac. She couldn't have. It took a scientist—a physical scientist, one who knew electronics." A pause, while Stone drew a deep breath. "That's why it has to be you, Mac. You're the man with the know-how. Even if Reva could have done it, you'd have had to pass on it, o.k. the construction; that's part of your base director's job."

"I see."

"You had the motive, too, Mac. And I understand it: When you found The Project was failing, you blew up, clutched at straws. Then the aliens came along and contacted you, somehow. They offered you their own special straw with a hook in it. Probably they promised that if you'd help them get krypton, they'd figure you a new angle on The Project. And you were so afraid of failing, washing up your career, that you grabbed at the chance. The hook—you were too eager to see it. After all, nobody on Earth knew that krypton was a catalyst, holding our atmosphere

together. How could you guess it?"

"Your logic's good, Carl." MacDougal nodded slowly. "You've done some straight thinking. But if what you say's true, then where does it leave us? I've made a mistake, but what have I done wrong?"

"You still don't see it?"

"I'm afraid not."

"Then I'll tell you." Stone sighed, just a little. "To you, Mac, your career's too important. If you think it's in danger, everything else has to get out of the way. Like here, now. You'd have had us kill Reva—to give you a goat, and keep me from talking. There'd be no black marks on your record. Maybe you even picked up a few tricks from the monsters that would make The Project go."

"So—?" The base director spoke very gently.

"So it won't wash, Mac. I'm security. It's my job to see straight, and to push out people whose careers mean more than duty."

"We've been friends a long time, Carl—"

It was Stone's turn to nod. "Thats' what makes it so hard, Mac. Maybe if the aliens come back, you'd have an H-bomb all waiting. Maybe. But maybe not, too. Maybe you'd bite on another hook—one that would really catch, give the monsters their chance to laugh and laugh and laugh, all the

way back to Arcturus Four—"
Stone broke off abruptly. "No,
Mac. We can't take that chance.
I'm sorry."

"I'm sorry, too, Carl." The heavy
shoulders shifted. "Because—it
means I have to kill you, as well as
Doctor Adams."

Stone frowned. "That might take
some doing."

"I doubt it." Of a sudden there
was ice in the base director's voice
—ice, and granite. His sling-sus-
pended hand moved sharply. "You
see, I've got a gun here, Carl. My
arm isn't really hurt, but the sling
seemed like good cover." He laughed, harsh and short. "Any last
words—?"

A numbness came to Stone's middle.

How far was he from MacDougal? Three steps? Four?

Too far.

He looked over at Reva.

SHE stood as before, still clutching her torn dress. The bulki-
ness of the fabric lumped in her
twisting fingers was like a deform-
ity growing out of her side. Strain
had stolen her face's last traces of
beauty. Her blonde hair hung limp
and straggly.

Stone didn't care. Of a sudden he
could think only of all the words
unspoken between them; of the
long years that should have been

theirs, the feelings crumbling down
into ashes.

Inside him, the emptiness swirled to a churning vortex. "Reva—!"
he whispered. "Reva . . ."

"Time's up!" MacDougal said.
His sling-hand flickered out.

Stone lunged at him.

Only it was too far, too far. He
knew it even as he charged. Mac-
Dougal's bullet would cut him down
in mid-stride.

And then Reva would die.
He sobbed a curse that came out
as a prayer.

MacDougal's gun leveled, rock-
steady.

Stone braced for the slug.

Only then—suddenly; incredibly
—another gun roared. A gun off
to one side, from where Reva stood.

MacDougal jerked round, firing
wildly.

With every ounce of his weight,
Stone crashed his fist against the
heavy, jutting jaw.

The base director's head snapped
back. Like a pole-axed ox, he top-
pled to the ground and lay there
motionless.

Stone picked up the gun and
stuck it into his belt. "Reva—"

She came to him, then—running,
arms out, the torn dress forgotten.

For a long moment, Stone held
her. "You . . . saved my life."

"With your own gun." Of a sudden, she was shaking. "It landed

beside me, back there on the sphere-ship. I hid it under my dress—for myself. I didn't want to die with tentacles around me . . ."

Her voice broke. She buried her face on Stone's shoulder. He held her close.

"We're not going to die," he said gently. "Neither of us. Not now. We've got too much to live for." Her face came up slowly. "To live for!" she echoed.

Never, Stone thought, had he seen her so beautiful.

Together, then, hand in hand, they walked out across the desert towards the distant highway.

THE END

"Well, that takes care of 10 years and 50 million dollars!"

Coffin For Two

by

Winston K. Marks

**He returned to Earth after three years,
with stars in his eyes and Gwen in his heart.
But Gwen had no heart — and a star on her brow!**

WHEN I saw the lights of Albany Field below me I just about cried. It takes guts to live anywhere by yourself for three years, but that itchy, stinking garden of hell out on Venus does things to you that aren't worth money. Not even the kind of money I'd get for the two tons of refined uranium concentrate I prospected out of Callispo Valley.

Well, that was all over, and I just sat there at the controls trying not to bawl. I set her down, gunned up to the Import Shed, checked in my cargo by short-wave — God, but that first voice sounded good, — and turned the 40-ton crate over to the Port Receiver. And then the first human eyes in three years watched me shake out fourteen inches of beard and climb down on good old U. S. A., Earth, dirt.

He was the surface jockey, a blond young man in a black jumper, and I almost hugged him I was so glad to see flesh and blood again. I was especially glad, although a little surprised they hadn't sent out one of those gangly robot jockeys they were beginning to use at the ports when I left for Venus. It would have been a hell of a homecoming, staring into those fish eyes for a welcoming committee.

I pumped his hand and said, "Boy, do you look good to me! How come no robots on duty around here? And what's the red star on your forehead for?"

"Welcome home, mister," he said. "You must have been out there for quite a while. You'll find things changed, I imagine. If you want I'll take over now."

Sure. Things were bound to be changed after three years. But not certain people, not Tommy and Alec and Forest and —and maybe

70

not even Gwendolyn. I didn't dare to expect that Gwen was still waiting for me, but I couldn't help hoping.

I knocked the glass out of a phone booth getting in and started punching coins into the slot. Tommy was out, but Alec answered and swore a grand welcome. He'd have the gang rounded up at his flat in two hours.

"I'll be there soon as I get my lawn mowed," I told him. "And say, how about, uh, is Gwen still around?"

"Of course. She'll be there." Just like that.

I noticed everyone on the taxi ramp wore red stars, five-pointed affairs about an inch across, right smack in the middle of their foreheads. Funny kind of a fad, I thought. Nobody had paid much attention to me around the Port, but when I got out of the cab at the Vilt Hotel I got long goings-over. The driver wore a red star. So did the hotel clerk, and a woman in an ermine wrap, and about nine-tenths of the people in the lobby. I stared as hard at them as they did at me.

I got a room and took a bath. Then, feeling self-conscious in my out-of-date clothes. I went down to the barbershop. Here I got a real

surprise. The barbers were barbers! The shoe-shine boy and the
porter were amiable looking dark-
ies!

He no more got the bib under
my chin than I asked, "What happened to all the robots? Not that I
prefer them, you understand. But
what's the score? I've been away,
and I thought —"
The barber grinned. "You must
have been away. I suppose you
mean those animated junk piles
three or four years ago. They're
gone. Nothing on the hoof but
Government issue now." Without
any comment he clapped a rubber
something over my nose and I
took a dive.

WHEN I woke up my beard
was on the floor, I was
trimmed, shaved, manicured and
shined. That being my first brush
with barbershop anaesthetic, now
I understood the sign on the mirror: WE FEATURE THE NEW
DREAM SERVICE. This new
wrinkle made me forget about the
robots. But one thing I did notice.
In this barbershop there were
only five chairs where they used to
have them strung out as far as you
could see. And there was something else that should have tipped
me off to the situation. All the
other four chairs were occupied by
fellows without red stars on their
faces.

But me, I was space-happy about
then with the prospect of seeing
Gwen and the gang, so I didn't
think any more of it at the time. I
caught an interurban Hedge-Hop-
per for New York and spent the
time wondering a game of she-
loves-me, she-loves-me-not.

Alec had done pretty well in two
hours. Almost everybody I knew in
New York State was jammed into
his apartment when I got there. I
looked around for Gwen. Forest
said she'd be along pretty soon.

She came in on Tommy's arm
looking about as sweet as the girl
you're still in love with can look.
She held out her arms and kissed
me, but there was a little too much
"Welcome home" in that hug, and
not enough "Gee, Bill, but I've
missed you!" to suit me. Tommy
didn't approve too much of what
she did give me, but he seemed
cordial enough at first.

So things were like that. Old,
Pal, Old Gal, and Absence Makes
the Heart Go Wander.

Gwen wasn't wearing a diamond,
so I said to myself, nuts, Tommy's
a nice guy, but he wasted too much
time. After awhile I got her alone
out on Alec's little balcony. It developed that Tommy had made
more headway than I figured. She
was pretty stand-offish at first.

I was just beginning to get somewhere when the door jerked open
behind us. Tommy saw me with my

arm around Gwen's shoulder. He looked mean, and that red star on his forehead made him look meaner.

"What's up, Tommy!" I asked.

"Your number's up if you don't lay off Gwen. She's my girl now."

"Hey, wait a minute," I said. "This is still America."

"Come on, Gwen." He took her arm and jerked. I was in no mood for that. I lined out a left jab across his bow. Somehow a fist got in my way. It was Tommy's fist, and I could feel a couple of bones in my hand crack when our knuckles met.

He said, "Go away!" giving me a little shove that almost dumped me over the railing for a six-story glide. By the time I got untangled Tommy had towed Gwen out of the flat.

I went back to the party almost as mad as I was curious. I collared Alec and asked him, "Since when did Tommy become an ironman? I used to toss him around like a sparrow. And incidentally what's all this red star business? It looks pretty silly to me."

Alec looked at me kind of funny. "You don't — know what the red star signifies?" I shook my head, and he frowned. "Look," he said, "let's have a party tonight, and I'll tell you all about it in the morning."

That was all right with me. This crowded flat was getting on my nerves, so I invited the whole mob into a fleet of cabs and went searching for some night life.

WE were barely out in the lights when a snubby little vehicle whammed out of a side-pass and just about pulverized our lead cab.

"Oh, that's too bad!" Alec said. "I think Forest and Kelly were in that one. They'll hate to miss this party."

"Too bad?" I shouted. "My God, is that all it is when a couple of your buddies get ground into a pudding? Look at that mess."

That's all our driver did, was to glance at the two smoking, half-fused lumps of machinery then swing out around them and back into traffic. Alec caught my arm.

"Take it easy, Bill. They're not hurt. That's all part of this new set-up. I guess I'd better tell you now."

I guessed he better had. My stomach was rising and about to shine. I said, "None of your super-surgery is going to do those boys any good. They're pulp!"

"Bill, there isn't a spot of real flesh and blood back there on the pavement, unless the cab driver was *fleshing it*, and damned few of them do." Just then the cab stopped. Alec shouted to the rest that we'd be back pretty soon. He turned on the dome-light and told the driver to cruise around.

Tapping his red star solemnly he said, "Bill, have you ever thought about *not dying* — ever?" He stuck out a bare hand. He cramped his fingers, wiggled them, pressed each against his thumb then grabbed my hand and gave it a squeeze. It felt warm and human until he put the pressure on. I got the sensation of being caught in a hydraulic vise. There was inhuman power in those slender fingers.

"Jab it and it'll jump. Cut it and it'll bleed. Freeze it and it would rot off if you didn't replace it. It's fifty per cent stronger and reacts with greater sensitivity and coordination than the hand I was born with."

I didn't understand yet, but I was getting disgusted already. Alec said, "Now keep your mind open a minute, Bill. Here, I'll show you some more." He bared the right half of his upper torso. Touching a spot in his armpit he laid open a flap of skin over his right breast. In a four-inch cubic cavity snuggled a red rubber lump with two tubular outlets that buried their opposite ends in his body. "That's the power pick-up. The sympathetic mechanism is in the skull."

I watched him rearrange his clothing. I said, "So the red star signifies a robot? So I've been on a party with a bunch of pretty synthetics? Okay, Mister Rubber-Liver, now tell me what happened to Alec. Where is he? DON'T tell me they cut his heart and brain out and stuck it in that phony flesh-pot. I don't believe it, and if you don't tell me where Alec is I'll scramble your cogs."

What I had been calling "Alec" laughed nervously and realistically. "You give me the same chills we all had when we first tried these *proxies* out. It does seem a bit ghastly at first, but it's all so perfect that you can't argue it down. Bill, I'm in two places at once. Right now my real body is back at my apartment in an indestructible — well, you won't like the word, but we call them coffins. Oh, very well, don't believe me. I'll show you, by heaven!"

We drove back to his apartment. I was so befuddled it didn't even seem strange when he told me to wait beside him while he stretched out full length in front of a closed door leading out of his kitchenette. He relaxed and then sagged even more, until he was motionless at my feet.

The door clicked an inch ajar behind me. Alec's voice yelled out *from the room.* "Wait a minute, Bill."

I wasn't waiting. I was finding out. I kicked the door open and found myself in a five-by-eight cell with just enough room for the narrow door to swing in and miss a sure-enough coffin. Only it was transparent, and the body in it was just lying down making itself comfortable. A white arm was reaching up to close the lid when the head turned and saw me.

It was Alec, all right, naked and looking kind of annoyed. "Dammit, Bill, I told you — well, it's no longer sterile in here, so come in." He shoved back the lid, got out and took a robe off a hook.

"Are you convinced now?" He grinned and stuck out his hand. I was convinced, but I wasn't happy about it.

"Yeah, I suppose so," I admitted, "but now that I'm here, how does it work?"

He put on the robe and reached down inside the coffin. "These two levers control the whole business. This one," he pressed it, "cuts in the proxy. When my head is between those electrode plates I'm in perfect rapport. Watch."

He bent into the coffin. I heard a shuffle on the kitchen floor, and in walked another Alec. I looked from one to the other. It wasn't a healthy sensation. I said, "Cut it out. One of you guys is enough at a time." The proxy lay down carefully, and Alec withdrew his head.

"This other lever controls the lamps and the gas." He moved it, and the glass box filled with a smoky blue light from tubes that ran the length of the inside edges. "That fog is an organic gas that seeps in at specific rate. It's mixed with oxygen, and when you inhale it your lungs absorb it directly into the blood stream. In the presence of this ultra-violet H light your body can utilize the stuff by photosynthesis. A shot of synthetic porphyrins once a month keeps up an abnormal sensitivity to light, and your blood stream manufactures enough carbohydrates to supply the minimum energy you use up lying prone and in your hour's exercise a day."

"Exercise?"

"Of course. There would be general atrophy of the whole body if you didn't flex your muscles once in awhile. This short-wave light keeps your organs toned up and inhibits infection. The whole room is sterilized once a day or whenever the door is opened. The door, incidentally, locks only on the inside."

"What," I asked, "would happen if I lay down in there?"

"Nothing. You'll have to have your own proxy molded and synchronized. They're one-man affairs."

"Whatever made you think I'd have one of those blasted things around impersonating me," I grouched.

"Hell, you're impossible. Get out of here. I'm going to sterilize this room."

I slammed out of the apartment before Alec's proxy came to life.

THE next morning I got Gwen on the phone. She was still a little cool, but she apologized. "It wasn't fair for Tommy to push you around while you were *fleshing it.* If you reported him he'd stand a stiff fine."

"He'll stand a carbon knock in his carburetor if he crosses me again," I promised her. "How about you and me at the Vilt Ballroom tonight — in the flesh?" I added. There was a little silence.

"You don't understand, Bill. We don't flesh it unless something serious happens to our proxies, and then only until they're repaired. Besides, you'd better stay away from me until your proxy is completed. Tommy has taken certain proprietary rights in me these days, and he's terribly jealous."

In my Sunday vocabulary I told her what the Government Health Bureau could do with their proxies. She took this as a reflection upon herself, which it more or less was, I guess. Anyway, she hung up on me.

The first thing, I decided, was to teach Tommy the Open Door Policy. I didn't want him butting in when I got in the swing with Gwen. I found his proxy at his office behind a lucite door labeled, ASSISTANT TRAFFIC MAN-AGER, Stratas Five.

"Tommy," I said, "for the sake of old times I won't pop you. But get this straight, next time you shove that plastic nose into my business your proxy'll be crying for a proxy. Incidentally, if you ever have guts enough to play paddy-cake for keeps, leave that super-stand-in at home and come see me."

Tommy smiled with a set of perfect, of course, teeth. "The trouble with you, Bill, is that you're in my office. Your flesh is stinking up the place. Get out."

"Tommy, stand up and defend yourself."

Tommy not only stood up but he slapped down my special one-two punch like an Oreus Bug-eater spanking flies. Then he threw me out.

This was getting not only monotonous but kind of painful. Now both hands ached, and I bled from minor lacerations I won't identify.

I got pretty interested watching them put my first proxy together that afternoon. It was much more complicated than I had thought. Only the skeletal structure was inanimate when brought into short-wave rapport. There was a heart and a regular bloodstream. They explained that a nervous system operates under more influences than afferent and efferent control impulses, and in order to give sensation and emotional reaction they had to include synthetic glands to release real secretions like adrenalin. Hence, they needed a bloodstream, which distributed the various juices and produced authentic reactions and adjustments to the emotional stimuli of the real body and the environmental conditions of the proxy.

It wasn't a bad experience at all. They even warmed the mud for the moulage cast, and and it felt kind of good mushing around in it until I got told to lie still. The first proof of the matrix showed every mole and hair on me, even the tiny insect scars I collected on Venus.

I was sitting there admiring the finished product — it's a funny sensation getting the first good look at the back of your neck — when a guy stepped up with a short-handled hammer and potted my poor proxy on the forehead. The damned indelible red star! It reminded me of certain aspects of second-hand living that had slipped my mind.

This ghoulish feeling got even stronger that night when I lay down in my new apartment, in my new cell, in my new coffin. Following directions, I had locked the door from the inside, stripped, sterilized the cell and pulled the transparent coffin lid down over me. The two levers jutted conveniently by my hand. I pushed the first one and had to close my eyes against the sharp H-light. A warm draft of sweetish gas drifted in, smelling like grass right after it's cut. The deadly silence and this smell reminded me of a cemetery. I noted my heart slow down, then I didn't seem to need such deep breaths. This was approaching the state of semi-suspended animation they had explained would lengthen a man's life span almost indefinitely.

When I pulled the second lever something seemed to jar my brain into a long tunnel full of mercury. At one end was this coffin affair and my earthly clay. The other end let out through the eyes of my proxy in the white laboratory of the Government Health Bureau eight miles away. After a few minutes of this mental ice-skating I decided to take over my understudy, which just required, apparently, a curious feeling as to what was going on at the other end of the line.

I stood my new container up on its feet and did a little experimental shadow-boxing. After a few minutes a blonde, red-star female came in and tossed me a towel to wipe off the salty scum of synthetic perspiration and said, "Nothing wrong with that build. It'll get you there and back. If you want to leave now, your clothes are in there."

The long mirror in the dressing room showed the one flaw in my proxy. I was *supposed* to be blushing.

BACK at the apartment I smeared some makeup over the red star. My Venusian complexion, which was still about the color of an old soccer ball, and which they had refused to improve in my proxy, made it easy to disguise the mark. It was a penitentiary offense I'd been told, but I wanted to find out something about Tommy.

Knowing that Gwen had a date with Tommy, I got there early. She let me in and then invited me to get out. "Tommy'll be here any minute," she told me, avoiding her star with a powder puff.

I said, "You almost look human in that purple outfit."

"Well, I don't want blood spattered all over it," she said. "Oh Bill, why didn't you get a proxy. I — I think a great deal of both of you. You're no match for Tommy's proxy. Tommy will kill you, then he'll be executed, then I'll throw away my proxy and let myself dry up to be an old maid."

"I don't quite get this Gwen. You've changed a lot. The Gwen I used to know hated a bully. You stand there and tell me that Tommy will use his proxy to mash me up in my skin, and still you're sweet on him."

She looked just a little embarrassed. "You aren't used to things yet, Bill. The ethics are changed. If you stay you'll be learing at Tommy and baiting him. You know what a temper he has."

"Well, my ethics haven't changed any," I said. "And personally, I doubt that you're right about Tommy. I like Tommy. We were pals. Sure he's got a temper, but if it's changed him into an adolescent maniac, then maybe you shouldn't be running around with him. Anyhow, we'll find out pretty soon."

"The hard way." She looked so bleak and concerned I knew she wasn't just feeling sorry for herself. The trouble was I couldn't be sure if it was Tommy or me she was really worried about.

I finally figured there was one way of finding out, but I got only half way to her when Tommy busted in. Very sweet he looked until he saw me.

I led off, "Hello, Pinocchio. Do you look smooth! Who takes the dents out of your fenders these days?" I was surprised to notice Gwen sit back in her chair, interested but not so fearful looking any more.

Tommy glared for a second, then he said, "You!"

"Right," I admitted. "I see your

headlights are adjusted, too. Well, if you people are going out for the evening, I guess I'll go home and rest up. See you tomorrow, Gwen."

Science is wonderful. They've even improved on a man's sneer. Tommy's lips twisted into something like what a pretzel-maker would dream about. Deep down in his rubber throat he said, "This is what you asked for."

I dived over the sofa and yelled, "Take it easy, you lug. What are you going to do?"

I let him catch me the third time around the sofa. He knocked down the few feeble cracks I took at him, then he got ahold of my throat. I wilted and waited. Here was the answer.

A proxy breathes, but only for the purpose of talking. All the vital arteries and nerve threads being buried good and deep, it was easy to let his fingers gouge in. All I felt was the surface pain which there was plenty of.

Just when my eyes were supposed to come popping out of my head I quit play-acting. I reached up and scrubbed my red star clean for Tommy to look at. "Leggo my tie," I commanded, and he did.

"That's — illegal!" he gagged. It was surprising how fast he cooled off. Of course he'd been meaning to break a rule or two himself, and it was only my Tro-

jan Horse in reverse that had stopped him.

He turned on Gwen and shouted, "That's a fine sweetheart you are! Why didn't you warn me?"

"Why Tommy, against what?" she asked innocently. "Besides, I didn't know for sure. I only guessed."

"I don't know what you can see in a Venusian mud mucker, but if you want him take him."

"Thank you," Gwen said. "Maybe it's his ethics I like. Don't bother dropping in at the wedding."

For a second I thought Tommy was going to throw his proxy into battle, but I guess he reconsidered the fact that with my proxy I had gotten back my old muscle ratio in proportion to his somewhat puny one. Knowing how hard he was going to take this jilt, I wouldn't even have kicked him in the pants if he hadn't used a dirty word on the way out.

Gwen shut the door after him and said, "He meant to kill you."

I asked her, "Were you serious about that wedding?"

"You just ruined the self- respect of my only other prospect. Do I have to get down on my hands and knees?"

"I guess that does leave me a clear field, doesn't it?"

She looked at me half smiling and half not smiling. "Well, Bill, what have I done to deserve all that enthusiasm? Come to think of it, this was my idea, wasn't it?"

Righ here I was supposed to say something and put it all right, but the something wouldn't come. Gwen came over and turned up her face. If those had been her real eyes they'd have had tears in them.

She said, "It looks like I stuck my neck out. Maybe I'll learn not to take a proxy for granted."

"That's just it," I managed to say. "I really wanted to marry you three years ago, and I still feel that way about the real — you. But I just can't get feeling like that about

a rubber doll even if it does look like you."

"Oh," she said and looked down so I couldn't see her face.

"Look, Gwen," I hesitated, then I blurted out, "How do these proxy people go about getting married?"

"Same as always. Hunt up a minister and take the vows."

"And — then what?" I insisted, and at that instant I made a discovery: *Lady* proxies can blush!

"And then you go out and buy a coffin for two," she murmured into my mangled necktie.

THE END

★ *Atomics At Sea* ... ★

THE successful application of atomic power plants to submarines and aircraft carriers is a triumph of technology. It introduces the concept of unlimited range. Atomic powered ships don't run out of fuel! That perhaps is the biggest advantage of all, for basically an atomic powered ship does not differ greatly in other respects from her more conventional equipped sister vessels.

The atomic engine merely replaces the boilers of the regular steam-turbine driven ship. Turbines still turn the propellors. The advantages come from greatly decreased weight (munitions and guns can take its place), the enormous ranges permitted and the relative simplicity of much of the engineering. The atomic reactors will of

course be shielded and armored so that a warship is less vulnerable from any kind of attack.

Most likely all future naval vessels of great size will be atomic powered. The appearance of such ships will not be altered very much though, since hull design has reached its theoretical peak. Only superstructures will change. There is one enigmatic change possible—eventually some ships will be driven by a water - jet system, also atomic powered. This is the outstanding hope for future speed increases. Water-jet propulsion apparently doesn't have the limitations of the ordinary propellor. Again Man imitates Nature—beetles have used the system for millenia!

* * *

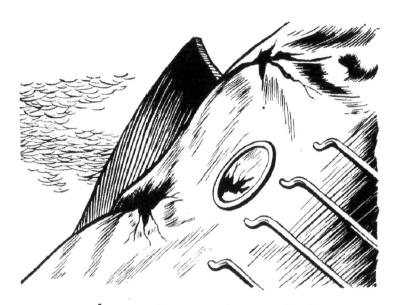

It was a dangerous planet—swallowing up
men with no apparent menace to fight against. It
was up to Allison and his computer to discover—

The Invisible Enemy

by

Jerry Sohl

FOR an hour they had been
circling the spot at 25,000
feet while technicians weighed
and measured the planet and electronic fingers probed where no eye
could see.

And for an hour Harley Allison
had sat in the computer room ac-
cepting the information and record-
ing it on magnetic tapes and
readying them for insertion into the
machine, knowing already what the

answer would be and resenting what the commander was trying to do.

It was quiet in the ship except for the occasional twitter of a speaker that recited bits of information which Allison dutifully recorded. It was a relief from the past few days of alarm bells and alerts and flashing lights and the drone of the commander's voice over the intercom, even as that had been a relief from the lethargy and mindlessness that comes with covering enormous stellar distances, for it was wonderful to see faces awaken to interest in things when the star drive went off and to become aware of a changing direction and the lessening velocity. Then had eyes turned from books and letters and other faces to the growing pinpoints of the Hyades on the scanners.

Then had Allison punched the key that had released the ship from computer control and gave it to manual, and in the ensuing lull the men of the *Nesbitt* were read the official orders by Commander William Warrick. Then they sat down to controls unmanned for so long to seek out the star among the hundreds in the system, then its fourth planet and, a few hours ago, the small space ship that lay on its side on the desert surface of the planet.

* * *

There was laughter and the

scrape of feet in the hall and Allison looked up to see Wendell Hallom enter the computer room, followed by several others.

"Well, looks like the rumors were right," Hallom said, eyes squinting up at the live screen above the control panel. The slowly rotating picture showed the half-buried space ship and the four pillars of the force field about it tilted at ridiculous angles. "I suppose you knew all about this, Allison."

"I didn't know any more than you, except we were headed for the Hyades," Allison said. "I just work here, too, you know."

"I wish I was home," Tony Lazzari said, rolling his eyes. "I don't like the looks of that yellow sand. I don't know why I ever joined this man's army."

"It was either join or go to jail," Gordon Bacon said.

"I ought to punch you right in the nose." Lazzari moved toward Bacon who thumbed his nose at him. "In fact, I got a good mind to turn it inside out."

Allison put a big hand on his shoulder, pulled him back. "Not in here you don't. I got enough troubles. That's all I'd need."

"Yeah," Hallom said. "Relax, kid. Save your strength. You're going to need it. See that pretty ship up there with nobody on it?"

"You and the commander," Bacon said. "Why's he got it in for you, Allison?"

"I wouldn't know," Allison said smiling thinly. "I've got a wonderful personality, don't you think?"

Hallom grunted. "Allison's in the Computer Corps, ain't he? The commander thinks that's just like being a passenger along for the ride. And he don't like it."

"That's what happens when you get an old line skipper and try to help him out with a guy with a gadget," Bacon observed.

"It wouldn't be so bad," Homer Petry said at the door, "if it had been tried before."

"Mr. Allison," a speaker blared.

"All right, you guys," Allison said. "Clear out." He depressed a toggle. "Yes, Lieutenant?"

"You have everything now, Allison. Might as well run it through."

"The commander can't think of anything else?"

There was a cough. "The commander's standing right here. Shall I ask him?"

"I'll run this right through, Lieutenant."

COMMANDER William Warrick was a fine figure of a man: tall, militant, greying, hatchet-nosed. He was a man who hewed so close to the line that he let little humanity get between, a man who would be perpetually young, for even at fifty there was an absence of paunch, though his eyes held a look of a man who had many things to remember.

He stood for a while at one end of the control room without saying anything, his never-absent map pointer in his right hand, the end of it slapping the open palm of his left hand. His cold eyes surveyed the men who stood crowded shoulder-to-shoulder facing him.

"Men," he said, and his deep voice was resonant in the room, "take a good look at the screen up there." And the eyes of nearly fifty men shifted to the giant screen beside and above him. "That's the *Esther*." The ship was on gyro, circling the spot, and the screen showed a rotation ship on the sand.

"We'll be going down soon and we'll get a better look. But I want you to look at her now because you might be looking at the *Nesbitt* if you're not careful."

The commander turned to look at the ship himself before going on. "The *Esther* is a smaller ship. It had a complement of only eight men. Remember the tense there. *Had*. They disappeared just as the men in the two ships before them did, each carrying eight men—the *Mordite* and the *Halcyon*. All three ships were sent to look for Traveen Abbott and Lew Gesell, two explorers for the Federation who had to their credit successful landings on more than ninety worlds. They were cautious, experienced and wise. Yet this planet swallowed them up. as it did the men of the three ships that followed."

Commander Warrick paused and looked at them severely. "We're fifty men and I think we have a better chance than an eight-man crew, not just because there are more of us but because we have the advantage of knowing we're against something really deadly. In case you haven't deduced our mission, it is simply to find out what it is and destroy it."

The insignia on the commander's collar and sleeve glittered in the light from the ever-changing screen as the ship circled the site of the *Esther*.

"This is a war ship. We are armed with the latest weapons. And—" his eyes caught Allison's "—we even have a man from the Computer Corps with us, if that can be counted as an advantage."

Allison who stood at the rear of the room behind the assembled soldier-technicians, reddened. "The tapes got us here, Commander."

"We could have made it without them," the commander said without ire. "But we're here with or without tape. But just because we are we're not rushing down there. We know the atmosphere is breathable, the gravity is close to Earth's and there are no unusually dangerous bacteria. All this came from the *Esther* prior to the . . .incident, whatever it was. But we checked again just to make sure. The gravity is nine-tenths that of Earth's, there is a day of twenty-four and a half hours, temperature and humidity tropical at this parallel, the atmosphere slightly less rich in oxygen, though not harmfully so—God only knows how a desert planet like this can have any oxygen at all with so little vegetation and no evident animal life. There is no dangerous radiation from the surface or from the sun. Mr. Allison has run the assembled data through his machine—would you care to tell the men what the machine had to say, Allison?"

Allison cleared his throat and wondered what the commander was driving at. "The planet could sustain life, if that's what you mean, Commander."

"But what did the machine say about the inhabitants, Mr. Allison?"

"There wasn't enough data for an assumption."

"Thank you. You men can get some idea of how the Computer Corps helps out in situations like this."

"That's hardly fair, Commander," Allison protested. "With more data—"

"We'll try to furnish you with

armsful of data." The commander smiled broadly. "Perhaps we might let you collect a little data yourself."

There was laughter at this. "So much for the Computer Corps. We could go down now, but we're circling for eighteen more hours for observation. Then we're going down. Slowly."

THE ship came out of the deep blue sky in the early morning and the commander was a man of his word. The *Nesbitt* moved down slowly, beginning at sun-up and ending in the sand within a few hundred feet of the *Esther* in an hour.

"You'd think," Lazzari said as the men filed back into the control room for another briefing, "that the commander has an idea he can talk this thing to death."

"I'd rather be talked to death by the commander than by you," Hallom said. "He has a pleasanter voice."

"I just don't like it, all that sand down there and nothing else."

"We passed over a few green places," Allison corrected. "A few rocky places, too. It's not all sand."

"But why do we have to go down in the middle of it?" Lazzari insisted.

"That's where the other ships went down. Whatever it is attack-ed them on the sand."

"If it was up to me, I'd say: Let the thing be, whatever it is. Live and let live. That's my motto."

"You're just lazy," said Petry, the thin-faced oldster from Chicago. "If we was pickin' apples you'd be askin' why. If you had your way you'd spend the rest of your life in a bunk."

"Lazy, hell!" Lazzari snorted. "I just don't think we should go poking our nose in where somebody's going to bite it off."

"That's not all they'll bite off, Buster," said Gar Caldwell, a radar and sonics man from Tennessee.

Wang Lee, force field expert, raised his thin oriental eyebrows and said, "It is obvious we know more than our commander. We know, for example, *it* bites. It follows then that it has teeth. We ought to report that to the commander."

The commander strode into the room, map pointer under his arm, bearing erect, shoulders back, head high. Someone called attention and every man stiffened but Allison, who leaned against the door. Commander Warrick surveyed them coldly for a moment before putting them at ease.

"We're dividing into five teams," he said. "Four in the field and the command team here. The rosters will be read shortly and duplicate equipment issued. The lieutenants know the plans and they'll explain them to you. Each unit will have a g-car, force field screen, television and radio for constant communication with the command team. There will be a blaster for each man, nuclear bombardment equipment for the weapons man, and so on."

He put his hands on his hips and eyed them all severely. "It's going to be no picnic. It's hot as hell out there. A hundred degrees in the daytime and no shade. It's eighty at night and the humidity's high. But I want you to find out what it is before it finds out what you are. I don't want any missing men. The Federation's lost three small ships and twenty-four men already. And Mr. Allison—"

Allison jerked from the wall at the unexpected calling of his name. "Yes, Commander?"

"You understand this is an emergency situation?"

"Well, yes, Commander."

The commander smiled slyly and Allison could read something other than humor behind his eyes.

"Then you must be aware that, under Federation regulations governing ships in space, the commander excercises unusual privileges regarding his crew and civilians who may be aboard."

"I haven't read the regulation, Commander, but I'll take your word for it that it exists."

"Thank you, Mr. Allison." The lip curled ever so slightly. "I'd be glad to read it to you in my quarters immediately after this meeting, except there isn't time. For your information in an emergency situation, though you are merely attached to a ship in an advisory capacity, you come under the jurisdiction of the ship's commander. Since we're short of men, I'm afraid I'll have to make use of you."

Allison balled two big, brown hands and put them behind his back. They had told him at Computer Corps school he might meet men like Commander Warrick— men who did not yet trust the maze of computer equipment that only a few months ago had been made mandatory on all ships of the *Nesbitt* class. It was natural that men who had fought through campaigns with the old logistics and slide-rule tactics were not going to feel immediately at home with computers and the men that went with them. It wasn't easy trusting the courses of their ships or questions of attack and defense to magnetized tape.

"I understand, Commander," Allison said. "I'll be glad to help· out in whatever way you think best."

"Good of you, I'm sure." The Commander turned to one of the lieutenants near him. "Lieutenant Cheevers, break out a blaster for Mr. Allison, He may need it."

WHEN the great port was opened, the roasting air that rushed in blasted the faces of the men loading the treadwagons. Allison, the unaccustomed weight of the blaster making him conscious of it, went with several of them down the ramp to look out at the yellow sand.

Viewing it from the surface was different from looking at it through a scanner from above. He squinted his eyes as he followed the expanse to the horizon and found there were tiny carpets of vegetation here and there, a few larger grass islands, a wooded area on a rise far away on the right, mountains in the distance on the left. And above it all was a deep blue sky with a blazing white sun. The air had a burned smell.

A tall lieutenant—Cork Rogers who would lead the first contingent—moved down the ramp into the broiling sun and gingerly stepped into the sand. He sank into it up to his ankles. He came back up, shaking his head. "Even the sand's hot."

Allison went down, the sun feeling like a hot iron on his back, bent over and picked up a handful of sand. It was yellower than Earth sand and he was surprised to find it had very little weight. It was more like sawdust, yet it was granular. He looked at several tiny grains closely, saw that they were hollow. They were easily crushed.

"Why was I born?" Lazzari asked no one in particular, his arms loaded with electrical equipment for the wagon. "And since I was, how come I ever got in this lousy outfit?"

"Better save your breath," Allison said, coming up the ramp and wiping his hands on his trousers. "Yeah, I know. I'm going to need it." He stuck his nose up and sniffed. "They call that air!"

In a few minutes, the first treadwagon loaded with its equipment and men purred down the ramp on its tracks and into the sand. It waited there, its eye tube already revolving slowly high on its mast above the weapons bridge. The soldier on the bridge was at ready, his tinted visor pulled down. He was actually in the small g-car which could be catapulted at an instant's notice.

Not much later there were four treadwagons in the sand and the commander came down the ramp, a faint breeze tugging at his sleeves and collar.

He took the salute of each of the officers in turn— Lieutenant Cork Rogers of Unit North, Lieutenant Vicky Noromak of Unit East, Lieutenant Glen Foster of Unit West and Lieutenant Carl Quartz of Unit South. They raised the green and gold of the Federation flag as he and the command team stood at attention behind him.

Then the commander's hand whipped down and immediately the purrs of the wagons became almost deafening as they veered from one another and started off through the sand, moving gracefully over the rises, churning powder wakes and leaving dusty clouds.

IT was quiet and cool in the control room. Commander Warrick watched the four television panels as they showed the terrain in panorama from out-positions a mile in each direction from the ship. On all of them there were these same things: the endless, drifting yellow sand with its frequent carpets of grass, the space ship a mile away, the distant mountain, the green area to the right.

Bacon sat at the controls for the panels, Petry at his side. Once every fifteen seconds a radio message was received from one of the tread-wagon units: "Unit West reporting nothing at 12:18:15." The reports droned out over the speaker system with monotonous regularity. Petry checked off the quarter minutes and the units reporting.

Because he had nothing better to do, Allison had been sitting in the control room for four hours and all he had seen were the television panels and all he had heard were the reports — except when Lieutenant Cheevers and three other men returned from an inspection of the *Esther*.

"Pile not taken, eh?" The commander pursed his lips and ran a forefinger along his jaw. "Anything above median level would have taken the pile. I can't see it being ignored."

The lieutenant shook his head. "The *Esther* was relatively new. That would have made her pile pretty valuable."

"I can't figure out why the eight men on the Esther couldn't handle the situation. They had the *Mordite* and the *Halcyon* as object lessons. They must have been taken by surprise. No sign of a struggle, eh, Cheevers?"

"None, sir. We went over everything from stem to stern. Force field was still working, though it had fallen out of line. We turned it off."

"No blood stains? No hair? No bones?"

"No, sir."

"That's odd, don't you think? Where could they have gone?" The commander sighed. "I expect we'll know soon enough. As it is, unless something is done, the *Esther* will sink farther into this sand until she's sunk out of sight with the other two ships." He frowned. "Lieutenant, how would you like to assume command of the *Esther* on our return? It must still be in working order if the pile is there. I'll give you a crew."

"We're not through here yet, sir." Cheevers grinned. "But I'd like it."

"Look good on your service records, eh, Corvin?" The commander then saw Allison sitting at the rear of the room watching the panels. "What do you make of all this, Allison?"

"I hardly know what to think, Commander."

"Why don't you run a tape on it?"

"I wish I could, but with what little we know so far it wouldn't do any good."

"Come, now, Allison, surely a good, man like you—you're a computer man, remember?— surely you could do something. I've heard of the wonders of those little machines. I'll bet you could run that through the machine and it will tell us exactly what we want to know."

"There's not enough data. I'd just get an ID—Insufficient Data—response as I did before."

"It's too bad, Allison, that the computer people haven't considered that angle of it— that someone has to get the data to feed the machine, that the Federation must still rely on guts and horse sense and the average soldier-technician. I'll begin thinking computers are a good thing when they can go out and get their own data."

THAT had been two hours ago. Two hours for Allison to cool off in. Two hours to convince himself it had been best not to answer the commander. And now they all sat, stony-faced and quiet, watching the never-ending sweep of the eye-tubes that never showed anything different except the changing shadows as the planet's only sun moved across the sky. Yellow sand and carpets of green, the ship, the mountain, the wooded area . . .

It was the same on the next four-hour watch. The eyetubes turned and the watchers in the ship watched and saw nothing new, and radio reports droned on every fifteen seconds until the men in the room were scarcely conscious of them.

And the sun went down.

Two moons, smaller than Earth's single moon, rode high in the sky, but they didn't help as much, infrared beams from the treadwagons rendered the panel pictures as plain as day. And there was nothing new.

The commander ordered the units moved a mile farther away the second day. When the action was completed, the waiting started all over again.

It would not be fair to say *nothing* was new. There was one thing—tension. Nerves that had been held ready for action began demanding it. And with the ache of taut nerves came impatience and an overexercising of the imagination. The quiet, heat, humidity and monotony of nothing the second day and night erupted in a blast from Unit East early on the morning of the third day. The nuclear weapons man in the g-car had fired at something he saw moving out on the sand.

At the site Technician Gar Caldwell reported by radio while Lieutenant Noromak and another man went through the temporarily damped force field to investigate. There was nothing at the target but some badly burned and fused sand.

Things went back to normal again.

Time dragged through the third day and night, and the hot breezes and high humidity and the waiting grated already raw nerves.

On the morning of the fourth day Homer Petry, who had been checking off the radio reports as they came in, suddenly announced: "No radio report from Unit West at 8:14:45!"

Instantly all eyes went to the Unit West panel.

The screen showed a revolving panorama of shimmering yellow sand and blue sky.

Lieutenant Cheevers opened the switch. "Unit West! Calling Unit West!"

No answer.

"What the hell's the matter with you, Unit West!"

The commander yelled, "Never mind, Lieutenant! Get two men and shoot over there. I'll alert the other units."

Lieutenant Cheevers picked up Allison, who happened to be in the control room at the time, and Hallom, and in a matter of moments the port dropped open and with the lieutenant at the controls and the two men digging their feet in the side stirrups and their hands clasping the rings for this purpose on either side, the small g-car soared out into the sweltering air and screamed toward Unit West.

The terrain rushed by below them as the car picked up still more speed and Allison, not daring to move his head too far from the protective streamlining lest it get caught in the hot airstream, saw the grass-dotted, sun-baked sand blur by.

Then the speed slackened and, raising his head, he saw the tread-wagon and the four force-field pillars they were approaching.

But he saw no men. .

The lieutenant put the car in a tight turn and landed it near the wagon. The three grabbed their weapons, jumped from the car and ran with difficulty through the sand to the site.

The force field blocked them.

"What the hell!" Cheevers kicked

at the inflexible, impenetrable shield and swore some more.

THE treadwagon was there in the middle of the square formed by the force field posts, and there was no one in it. The eye-tube was still rotating slowly and noiselessly, weapons on the bridge beneath still pointed menacingly at the empty desert, the g-car was still in its place, and the Federation flag fluttered in the slight breeze.

But there was nothing living inside the square. The sand was oddly smooth in many places where there should have been footprints and Allison wondered if the slight breeze had already started its work of moving the sand to obliterate them. There were no bodies, no blood, no signs of a struggle.

Since they couldn't get through the barrier, they went back to the g-car and went over it, landing inside the invisible enclosure, still alert for any emergency.

But nothing attacked because there was nothing there. Only the sand, the empty treadwagons, the weapons, the stores.

"Poor Quartz," Cheevers said.

"What, sir?" Hallom asked.

"Lieutenant Quartz. I knew him better than any of the others." He picked up a handful of sand and threw it angrily at the wagon's treads.

Allison saw it hit, watched it fall, then noticed the tread prints were obliterated inside the big square. But as he looked out across the waste to the ship he noticed the tread prints there were quite clear.

He shivered in the hot sun.

The lieutenant reported by the wagon's radio, and after they had collected and packed all the gear, Allison and Hallom drove the treadwagons back to the ship.

"I tell you it's impossible!" The commander's eyes were red-rimmed and bloodshot and he ran sweating hands through wisps of uncombed grey hair. "There must have been *something!*"

"But there wasn't, sir," Cheevers said with anguish. "And nothing was overlooked, believe me."

"But how can that be?" The commander raised his arms angrily, let them fall. "And how will it look in the record? Ten men gone. Just like that." He snapped his fingers. "The Federation won't like it—especially since it is exactly what happened to the others. If only there had been a fight! If there were a chance for reprisal! But this—" he waved an arm to include the whole planet. "It's maddening!"

It was night before the commander could contain himself enough to talk rationally about what had happened and to think creatively of possible action.

"I'm not blaming you, Lieutenant Cheevers, or anybody," he said slouched in his desk chair and idly eying the three remaining television screens that revealed an endless, turning desert scene. "I have only myself to blame for what happened." He grunted. "I only wish I knew what happened." He turned to Cheevers, Allison and Hallom, who sat on the other side of the desk. "I've done nothing but think about this thing all day. I don't know what to tell those fellows out there, how they can protect themselves from this. I've examined the facts from every angle, but I always end up where I started." He stared at Cheevers. "Let's hear your idea again, Cheevers."

"It's like I say, sir. The attack could have come from the air."

"Carried away like eagles, eh? You've still got that idea?"

"The sand was smooth, Commander. That would support the idea of wings of birds setting the air in motion so the sand would cover up the footprints."

THE commander bit his lower lip, drummed on the desk with his fingers and stared hard at Cheevers. "It *is* possible. Barely possible. But it still doesn't explain why we see no birds, why we saw no birds on the other viewers during the incident, why the other teams saw no birds in flight. We've asked, remember? Nobody has seen a living thing. Where then are we going to get enough birds to carry off ten men? And how does this happen with no bloodshed? Surely one of our men could have got off one shot, could have wounded *one* bird."

"The birds could have been invisible, sir," Hallom said hesitantly.

"Invisible birds!" The commander glared. Then he shrugged. "Hell I suppose anything is possible."

"That's what Allison's machine says."

"I ran the stuff through the computer," Allison said.

"I forgot there was such a thing . . . So that's what came out, eh?"

"Not exactly, Commander." Allison withdrew a roll of facsimile tape. "I sent through what we had. There are quite a few possibilities." He unrolled a little of it. "The men could still exist at the site, though rendered invisible—"

"Nuts!" the commander said. "How the hell—!"

"The data," Allison went on calmly, "was pretty weird itself and the machine lists only the possibilities, taking into consideration everything no matter how absurd. Other possibilities are that we are victims of hypnosis and that we are to see only what *they*—whoever *they* are—want us to see; that the men were surprised and spirited away by something invisible, which would mean none of the other units would have seen or reported it; or that the men themselves would not have seen the—let's say 'invisible birds'; that the men sank into the sand somehow by some change in the composition of the ground itself, or were taken there by something, that there was a change in time or space—"

"That's enough," the commander snapped. He rose, eyes blazing. "I can see we're going to get nothing worthwhile from the Computer Corps. 'Change in Time' hell! I want a straight answer, not a bunch of fancies or something straight from a fairy tale. The only thing you've said so far I'd put any stock in is the idea of the birds. And the lieutenant had that idea first. But as far as their being invisible is concerned, I hardly think that's likely."

"But if it had been just birds," Allison said, putting away the roll of tape, "there would have been resistance and blood would have been spilled somewhere."

Commander Warrick snorted. "If there'd been a fight we'd have seen some evidence of it. It was too quick for a fight, that's all. And I'm warning the other units of birds and of attack without warning."

As a result, the three remaining units altered the mechanism of their eye-tubes to include a sweep of the sky after each 360 degree pan of the horizon.

The fourth night passed and the blazing sun burst forth the morning of the fifth day with the situation unchanged except that anxiety and tension were more in evidence among the men than ever before. The commander ordered sedatives for all men coming off watches so they could sleep.

The fifth night passed without incident.

It was nearly noon on the sixth day when Wang Lee, who was with Lieutenant Glenn Foster's Unit West, reported that one of the men had gone out of his head.

The commander said he'd send over a couple men to get him in a g-car.

But before Petry and Hollam left, Lee was on the radio again. "It's Prince, the man I told you about," he said. "Maybe you can see him in the screen. He's got his blaster out and insists we turn off the force field."

The television screen showed the sky in a long sweep past the sun down to the sand and around, sweeping past the figure of a man, obviously Prince, as it panned the horizon.

"Lieutenant Foster's got a blaster on him," Lee went on.

"Damn it!" Sweat popped out on the commander's forehead as he looked at the screen. "Not enough trouble without that." He turned to Cheevers. "Tell Foster to blast him before he endangers the whole outfit."

But the words were not swift enough. The screen went black and the speaker emitted a harsh click.

IT was late afternoon when the treadwagon from Unit West purred to a stop beside the wagon from Unit South and Petry and Bacon stepped out of it.

"There she is," Cheevers told the commander at his side on the ramp. "Prince blasted her but didn't put her out of commission. Only the radio—you can see the mast has been snapped off. No telling how many men he got in that blast before . . ."

"And now they're all gone. Twenty men." The commander stared dumbly at the wagon and his shoulders slouched a little now. He looked from the wagon to the horizon and followed it along toward the sun, shading his squinting red eyes. "What is it out there, Cheevers? What are we up against?"

"I wish I knew, sir."

They walked down the ramp to the sand and waded through it out to the treadwagon. They examined it from all sides.

"Not a goddam bloodstain anywhere," the commander said, wiping his neck with his handkerchief. "If Prince really blasted the men there ought to be stains and hair and remains and stench and—well, *something*."

"Did Rogers or Noromak report anything while I was gone?"

"Nothing. Not a damned thing . . . Scene look the same as before?"

"Just like before. Smooth sand inside the force field and no traces, though we did find Prince's blaster. At least I think it's his. Found it half-buried in the sand where he was supposed to be standing. We can check his serial number on it."

"Twenty men!" the commander breathed. He stared at the smooth sweep of sand again. "Twenty men swallowed up by nothing again." He looked up at the cloudless sky. "No birds, no life, no nothing. Yet something big enough to . . ." He shook his fist at the nothingness. "Why don't you show yourself, whoever you are—whatever you are! Why do you sneak and steal men!"

"Easy, Commander," Cheevers said, alarmed at the commander's red face, wide eyes and rising voice.

The commander relaxed, turned to the lieutenant with a wry face. "You'll have a command some day, Corvin. Then you'll know how it is."

"I think I know, sir," he said quietly.

"You only think you know. Come on, let's go in and get a drink. I need one. I've got to send in another report."

IF it had been up to Allison, he would have called in the two remaining units—Unit East, Lieutenant Noromak's outfit, and Unit North, Lieutenant Rogers' group—because in the face of what had twice proved so undetectable and unpredictable, there was no sense in throwing good men after those who had already gone. He could not bear to think of how the men felt who manned the remaining outposts. Sitting ducks.

But it was not up to him. He could only run the computer and advise. And even his advice need not be heeded by the commanding officer whose will and determination to discover the planet's threat had become something more to pity than admire because he was willing to sacrifice the remaining two units rather than withdraw and consider some other method of attack.

Allison saw a man who no longer looked like a soldier, a man in soiled uniform, unshaven, an irritable man who had spurned eating and sleeping and had come to taking his nourishment from the bottle, a man who now barked his orders in a raucous voice, a man who could stand no sudden noises and, above all, could not tolerate any questions of his decisions. And so he became a lonely man because no one wanted to be near him, and he was left alone to stare with fascination at the two remaining TV panels and listen to the half-minute reports . . . and take a drink once in a while.

Allison was no different from the others. He did not want to face the commander. But he did not want to join the muttering soldiers in crew quarters either. So he kept to the computer room and, for something to do, spliced the tapes he had made from flight technician's information for their homeward flight. It took him more than three hours and when he was finished he put the reels in the flight compartment and, for what he thought surely must have been the hundredth time, took out the tapes he had already made on conditions and factors involved in the current emergency. He rearranged them and fed them into the machine again, then tapped out on the keys a request for a single factor that might emerge and prove helpful.

He watched the last of the tape whip into the machine, heard the gentle hum, the click of relays and watched the current indicators in the three different stages of the machine, knew that inside memory circuits were giving information, exchanging data, that other devices were examining results, probing for other related information, extracting useful bits, adding this to the stream, to be rejected or passed, depending upon whether it fitted the conditions.

At last the delivery section was energized, the soft ding of the response bell and the lighted green bar preceded a moment when the answer facsimile tape whirred out and even as he looked at it he knew, by its length, that it was as evasive and generalized as the information he had asked it to examine.

He had left the door to the computer room open and through it suddenly came the sound of hoarse voices. He jumped to his feet and ran out and down the hall to the control room.

The two television panels showed nothing new, but there was an excited radio voice that he recognized as Lieutenant Rogers'.

"He's violent, Commander, and there's nothing we can do," the lieutenant was saying. "He keeps running and trying to break through the force field—oh, my God!"

"What is it?" the commander cried, getting to his feet.

"He's got his blaster out and he's saying something."

The commander rushed to the microphone and tore it from Cheevers's hands. "Don't force him to shoot and don't you shoot, Lieutenant. Remember what happened to Unit West."

"But he's coming up to the wagon now—"

"Don't lose your head, Rogers! Try to knock him out—*but don't use your blaster!*"

"He's entering the wagon now, Commander."

There was a moment's silence.

"He's getting into the g-car, Commander! We can't let him do that!"

"Knock him out!"

"I think we've got him—they're tangling—several men—he's knocked one away—he's got the damned thing going!"

There was a sound of clinking metal, a rasp and scrape and the obvious roar of the little g-car.

"He got away in it! Maybe you can pick it up on the screen . . ."

The TV screen moved slowly across the sky and swept by a g-car that loomed large on it.

"Let him go," the commander said. "We'll send you another. Anybody get hurt?"

"Yes, sir. One of the men got a bad cut. They're still working on him on the sand. Got knocked off the wagon and fell into the sand. I saw his head was pretty bloody a moment ago before the men gathered around him and . . . *my God! No! No!*"

"What!"

"*They're coming out of the*

ground—"

"What?"

There were audible hisses and clanks and screams and . . . and suddenly it was quiet.

"Lieutenant! Lieutenant Rogers!" The commander's face was white. "Answer me, Lieutenant, do you hear? Answer me! You—you can't do this to me!"

But the radio was quiet.

But above, the television screen showed a panorama of endless desert illuminated by infra red and as it swept by one spot Allison caught sight of the horrified face of Tony Lazzari as the g-car soared by.

ALLISON pushed the shovel deep into the sand, lifted as much of it as he could get in it, deposited it on the conveyor. There were ten of them digging in the soft yellow sand in the early morning sun, sweat rolling off their backs and chins—not because the sand was heavy or that the work was hard but because the day was already unbearably hot—digging a hole that couldn't be dug. The sand kept slipping into the very place they were digging. They had only made a shallow depression two or three feet deep at the most and more than twenty feet wide.

They had found nothing.

Commander Warrick, who stood in the g-car atop Unit North's treadwagon, with Lieutenant Noromak and Lieutenant Cheevers at his side, had first ordered Unit East to return to the ship, which Allison considered the smartest thing he had done in the past five days. Then a group of ten, mostly men who had not been in the field, were dispatched in Unit South's old wagon, with the officers in the g-car accompanying them, to Unit North.

There was no sign of a struggle, just the smooth sand around the wagon, the force field still intact and functioning.

Then the ten men had started digging . . .

"All right," the commander called from the wagon. "Everybody out. We'll blast."

They got out of the hole and on the other side of the wagon while the commander ordered Cheevers to aim at the depression.

The shot was deafening, but when the clouds of sand had settled, the depression was still there with a coating of fused sand covering it.

Later, when the group returned to the ship, three g-car parties were sent out to look for Lazzari. They found him unconscious in the sun in his g-car in the sand. They brought him back to the ship where he was revived.

"What did you see?" the commander asked when Lazzari regained consciousness.

Lazzari just stared.

Allison had seen men like this before. "Commander," he said, "this man's in a catatonic state. He'd better be watched because he can have periods of violence."

The commander glared. "You go punch your goddamn computer, Mr. Allison. I'll handle Lazzari."

And as the commander questioned the man, Lazzari suddenly started to cry, then jerked and, wild-eyed, leaped for the commander.

They put Lazzari in a small room.

Allison could have told the commander that was a mistake, too, but he didn't dare.

And, as the commander was planning his next moves against the planet's peril, Lazzari dashed his head against a bulkhead, fractured his skull, and died.

THE funeral for Lazzari the commander said, was to be a military one—as military as was possible on a planet revolving around a remote star in the far Hyades. Since rites were not possible for the twenty-nine others of the *Nesbitt* who had vanished, the commander said Lazzari's would make up for the rest.

Then for the first time in a week men had something else to think about besides the nature of things on the planet of the yellow sand that had done away with two explorers, the crews of three ships and twenty-nine Federation soldier-technicians who had come to do battle.

New uniforms were issued, each man showered and shaved, Lieutenant Cheevers read up on the burial service, Gordon Bacon practiced *Taps* on his bugle, Homer Petry gathered some desert flowers in a g-car, and Wendell Hallom washed and prepared Lazzari for the final rites which were to be held within a few hundred feet of the ship.

Though Allison complied with the directives, he felt uneasy about a funeral on the sand. He spent the hour before the afternoon services in the computer room, running tapes through the machine again, seeking the factor responsible for what had occurred.

He reasoned that persons on the sand were safe as long as the onslaught of the *things* out of the ground was not triggered by some action of men in the parties.

He did not know what the Unit South provocation had been—the radio signals had just stopped. He did know the assault on Unit West occurred after Prince's blast at the men on the treadwagon (though the blast in the sand at Unit North had brought nothing to the surface —if one were to believe Lieutenant Roger's final words about *things* coming out of the ground).

And the attack at Unit North was fomented by Lazzari's taking off in the g-car and throwing those battling him to the sand.

Allison went so far as to cut new tapes for each incident, adding every possible detail he could think of. Then he inserted these into the machine and tapped out a question of the advisability of men further exposing themselves by holding a burial service for Lazzari in the sand.

In a few moments the response whirred out.

He caught his breath because the message was so short. Printed on the facsimile tape were these words:

Not advised.

Heartened by the brevity of the message and the absence of all the ifs, ands and buts of previous responses, he tapped out another question: Was there danger to life?

Agonizing minutes. Then:

Yes.

Whose life?

All.

Do you know the factor responsible for the deaths?

Yes.

He cursed himself for not realizing the machine knew the factor and wished he had asked for it instead. With his heart tripping like a jackhammer, Allison tapped out: What is the triggering factor?

When the answer came he found it ridiculously simple and wondered why no one had thought of it before. He stood staring at the tape for a long time knowing there could now be no funeral for Tony Lazzari.

He left the computer room, found the commander talking to Lieutenant Cheevers in the control room. Commander Warrick seemed something of his old self, attired in a natty tropical, clean shaven and with a military bearing and a freshness about him that had been missing for days.

"Commander," Allison said. "I don't mean to interrupt, but—we can't have the funeral."

THE commander turned to him with a look full of suspicion. Then he said, "Allison, this is the one and only trip you will ever make with me. When we get back it will be either you or me who gets off this ship for the last time. If you want to run a ship you have to go to another school besides the one for Computer Corps men."

"I've known how you feel, Commander," Allison said, "and—"

"The General Staff ought to know that you can't mix army and civilian. I shall make it a point to register my feelings on the matter when we return."

"You can tell them what you

wish, Commander, but it so happens that I've found out the factor responsible for all the attacks."

"And it so happens," the commander said icily, "that the lieutenant and I are reviewing the burial rites. A strict military burial has certain formalities which cannot be overlooked, though I don't expect you to understand that. There is too little time to go into any of your fancy theories now."

"This is no theory, Commander. It's a certainty."

"Did your computer have anything to do with it?"

"It had everything to do with it. I'd been feeding the tapes for days—"

"While we're on the subject, Allison, we're not using computer tapes for our home journey. We're going the whole way manually. I'm awaiting orders now to move off this God-forsaken world, in case you want to know. I'm recommending it as out-of-bounds for all ships of the Federation. And I'm also recommending that computer units be removed from the *Nesbitt* and from all other ships."

"You'll never leave this planet if you have the funeral." Allison said heatedly. "It will be death for all of us."

"Is that so?" The commander smiled thinly. "Courtesy of your computer, no doubt. Or is it that you're afraid to go out on the sand again?"

"I'm not afraid of the sand, Commander. I'll go out any time. But it's the others I'm thinking of. I won't go out to see Lazzari buried because of the blood on his head and neither should anyone else. You see, the missing factor— the thing that caused all the attacks—is blood."

"Blood?" The commander laughed, looked at Cheevers, who was not laughing, then back at Allison. "Sure you feel all right?"

"The blood on Lazzari, Commander. It will trigger another attack."

"What about the blood that's in us, Allison? That should have prevented us from stepping out to the sand without being attacked in the first place. Your reasoning —or rather your computer's reasoning—is ridiculous."

"It's fresh blood. Blood spilled on the sand."

"It seems to me you've got blood on the brain. Lazzari was a friend of yours, wasn't he, Allison?"

"That has nothing to do with it."

The commander looked at him hard and long, then turned to the lieutenant. "Cheevers, Allison doesn't feel very well. I think he'd better be locked up in the computer room until after the funeral."

Allison was stunned. "Commander—!"

"Will you please take him away at once, Lieutenant? I've heard all I want from him."

Sick at heart, Allison watched the commander walk out of the control room.

"You coming along, Allison?" Cheevers asked.

Allison looked at the lieutenant. "Do you know what will happen if you go out there?" But there was no sympathy or understanding in the eyes of the officer. He turned and walked down the hall to the computer room and went in.

"It doesn't make any difference what I think," Cheevers said, his hand on the knob of the door, his face not unkind. "You're not in the service. I am. I have to do what the commander says. Some day I may have a command of my own. Then I'll have a right to my own opinion."

"You'll never have a command of your own . . . after today."

"Think so?" It seemed to Allison that the lieutenant sighed a little. "Goodbye, Allison."

It was an odd way to put it. Allison saw the door close and click shut. Then he heard the lieutenant walk away. It was quiet.

ANGUISH in every fiber, Allison clicked on the small screen above the computer, turned a knurled knob until he saw the area of the intended burial. He hated to look at what he was going to see. The eye of the wide, shallow grave stared at him from the viewplate.

In a few minutes he saw Bacon carrying a Federation flag move slowly into view, followed by six men with blasters at raise, then Hallom and his bugle, Lieutenant Cheevers and his book, the stretcher bearing Lazzari with three pallbearers on either side, and the rest of the men in double ranks, the officers leading them.

Go ahead Commander. Have your military field day because it's one thing you know how to do well. It's men like you who need a computer . . .

The procession approached the depression, Bacon moving to one side, the firing party at the far side of the shallow, Lieutenant Cheevers at the near end, making room for the pallbearers who moved into the depression and deposited their load there. The others moved to either side of the slope in single file.

Make it slick, Commander. By the numbers, straight and strong, because it's the last thing you'll ever do . . .

The men suddenly stiffened to attention, uncovering and holding their dress hats over their left breasts.

Bacon removed the Federation flag from its staff, draped it neatly over Lazzari. Cheevers then moved to the front and conducted the services, which lasted for several minutes.

This is the end, Commander . . .

Allison could see Commander Warrick facing the firing party, saw the blast volleys. But he was more interested in Lazzari. Two soldiers were shoveling the loose sand over him. Hallom raised his bugle to his lips.

Then *they* came.

Large, heavy, white porpoise-like creatures they were, swimming up out of the sand as if it were water, and snatching men in their powerful jaws, rending and tearing—clothes and all—as they rose in a fury of attacks that whipped up sand to nearly hide the scene. There were twenty or more and then more than a hundred rising and sinking and snapping and slashing, sun glistening on their shiny sides, flippers working furiously to stay atop the sand.

This, then, was the sea and these were the fish in it, fish normally disinterested in ordinary sweating men and machines and treadwagons, but hungry for men's blood or anything smeared with it—so hungry that a drop of it on the sand must have been a signal conducted to the depths to attract them all.

And when the men were gone there were still fish-like creatures burrowing into the sand, moving through it swiftly half in and out like sharks, seeking every last vestige of — blood.

Then as suddenly as they had come, the things were gone.

Then there was nothing but smooth sand where before it had been covered by twenty men with bowed heads . . . except one spot which maximum magnification showed to be a bugle half-buried in the sand.

ALLISON did not know how long he sat there looking at the screen, but it must have been been an hour because when he finally moved he could only do so with effort.

He alone had survived out of fifty men and he—the computer man. He was struck with the wonder of it.

He rose to leave the room. He needed a drink.

Only then did he remember that Cheevers had locked him in.

He tried the door.

It opened!

Cheevers *had* believed him, then. Somehow, this made the whole thing more tragic . . . there might have been others who would have believed, too, if the commander had not stood in the way . . .

The first thing Allison did was close the great port. Then he hunted until he found the bottle he was looking for. He took it to the computer room with him, opened the flight compartment, withdrew the tapes, set them in their proper slots and started them on their way.

Only when he heard the ship tremble alive did he take a drink . . .A long drink.

There would have to be other bottles after this one. There *had* to be. It was going to be a long, lonely ride home.

And there was much to forget.

THE END

"A primitive race, apparently—no shoes!"

It has been said that what a man does not understand he hates. Turesco felt that way about mutants. So he asked Remington to help destroy—

The Brat

by

Henry Slesar

THE brat came flying out of the doorway, just preceding the tip of a heavy farmer's boot. He scrambled down the short flight of wooden steps, fell to his knees and was up in a flash and racing around the corner of the house.

The farmer followed in a plodding run, swearing loudly and waving a blunt-edged shovel. But the brat was too quick and too clever. At the back of the house, he dropped to the ground and skittered under the raised building, into the concealment of the shadows. He saw the man stride past, his mud-crusted boots thrashing through the high grass. The farmer swore again. Then he completed his circuit of the house and went up the steps to his wife.

The brat listened.

"Trustin' everybody!" the far-mer was shouting. "There ain't no-body you won't trust! He might of been a thief, for all you know. And you feedin' him!"

"He was just a little boy," came the patient voice of his wife. "Just a boy who was lost."

"How did a kid get lost way out here?"

"I don't know. He was hungry."

"Sure he was hungry! But for all you know he might have —"

The brat tuned out their voices.

The grass under the house was soft, and even a little warm. It was nice, just lying there, tuning out all sounds.

All sounds, but not the smells. The brat smelled food — hot dumplings and frying chicken, siz-zling in bacon grease. The farmer was at his meal, and the brat was hungry.

He rolled over on his stomach

and tuned in the sounds again, but this time the voices had stopped and all he could hear were the friendly chirpings of the insects. He plucked a handful of the tall grass and put the ends into his mouth, chewing thoughtfully, his eyebrows a sharp V in the middle of his broad forehead.

A grasshopper leaped into a spot two inches from his elbow.

The brat regarded it intently, and then said: "Hello."

"Hello," said the grasshopper.

"Where are you going?"

"Hello," said the grasshopper. Then with a bound, he was out of reach and hopping in the sunlight.

The brat was disappointed. He looked around. Sure enough, another grasshopper appeared out of the clump near his feet. The brat raised himself carefully, and with a lightning motion, captured the insect in his fist. He held it up close to his eyes.

"Hello," he said.

The grasshopper squeaked.

"Where are you going?" asked the brat.

"OVER THERE!" cried the insect, and with a mighty leap, escaped the brat's fist and went bounding off in the same direction as the first.

The brat suddenly realized that all the grasshoppers beneath the farmhouse were emerging from their shaded resting spots and were heading for some sort of special place.

"WARD Remington, Protector First Class." The sec-

107

retary made the announcement, then she turned and went out.

The man behind the desk was fat, forty-five, and his face was strangely familiar. He rolled a cigar between his thumb and forefinger as lightly as if it had been a toothpick. His name was Turesco. At least, that was the name on the desk plaque. Alfred G. Turesco. But Ward thought he had another name, more familiar, like his face.

"Oh, yes!" said the fat man. "Protector Remington! Please come in!"

"Mr. Turesco—"

"Let's start off right. Call me Al. And I'll call you Ward. All right?"

"Ward nodded. "All right." He took a seat and said: "Shall we get on with it?"

"Something to drink first?" Turesco's plump fingers reached for a decanter on his desk. Ward waved them away. The fat man shrugged, sat down and lit his cigar. From a manilla folder he brought out a neat manuscript.

"History first?"

Ward said: "What?"

"The history of the case. Shall I review it?"

"Please."

"All right." He re-settled his bulk firmly in the leather chair, placed his cigar carefully on a tray, and began to read.

"'In the year 2040, Dr. Benja-min Lake returned from the Second Interstellar Expeditionary Flight, accompanied by a native of the Twin Planet Gemini, the first approximation of terrestrial life discovered in the galaxy. His name was Ars Tenz Li, and his physiological resemblance to the human organism was considered remarkable.'"

Turesco looked up for a moment, picked up his cigar and took a long puff. When he returned to the folio, his voice lost its formal tone — and appropriately so, for the manuscript, too, lost its air of impartial formality with the next words.

Ars Tenz Li was a tall gray-skinned, rather repulsive creature with an elongated skull, on the forehead of which grew four long antennae. He spoke no English, and demonstrated no desire to learn the language. The great majority of people were suspicious of his actions and intentions.

"'When Dr. Lake died of pulmonary thrombosis in September of that year, the Geminite mysteriously disappeared.

"'In March of the year 2045, a Nebraskan air pilot reported seeing the gray man plowing up farmland in the hill country of Colorado.

"'The Committee for Human Advancement sent its investigator to the area, where he learned the shocking fact that Ars Tenz Li had taken unto himself a wife. Prompt action enabled the Committee to free the woman, whose name was Bess Marshall. She was taken, although against her will, to Central City. The Committee felt no compunction in taking her from the Geminite, despite her objections, since she obviously had been influenced through hypnosis or other means, by the Geminite.

"Ars Tenz Li followed immediately, and demanded of the police of the city that his wife be found and returned to him. He now spoke perfect English.' "

THE FAT MAN glanced up again. Ward had been staring at his moving lips with a strange fascination.

Turesco said: "The rest, you probably know. The police found that the Geminite and the Marshall girl had been 'legally' married, and the records duly entered with the County Clerk in the little community they had settled in. However, our lawyer contested the 'legality' of this marriage, since the Geminite—although the late Dr. Lake had managed to have him declared an 'honorary' American citizen—was not truly human, and therefore, not liable unto the laws of the country, state, or city."

Ward fingered his visor. "And you lost," he said.

The fat man scowled, his lips working. "Yes. We lost. The judge voted the marriage legal. Ars Tenz Li went back to the farm with his wife."

Ward examined the man's face. Familiar.

"After that," he was saying, "they remained there for some ten years, and then—well, you know what happened."

"The lynching."

"Yes. Most unfortunate."

The Protector said: "Was it?"

Turesco's head jerked forward, a strange light in his eyes. "Don't you think so?" he asked.

Ward relaxed. "I guess so."

"Oh." The fat man mopped his brow with his open palm. "Well, that ended it. The folks in the community had been having some hard times, but somehow, the Geminite had managed to keep his farm prosperous. A crazy mob, a couple of drunken instigators, and the Geminite died on the rope. The CHA closed its book on the case."

"And now it's open again. Is that it?"

Turesco leaned back. "Yes," he replied. "It's open again." He took some glossy photo prints from the bottom of the manuscript and handed it to the protector.

Ward looked. It was a picture of a dead child on a slab. The body was horribly decomposed. But there was something else, something different. It was a tall child, taller than seemed right for its age, which appeared to be seven or eight. And the skull was elongated. And there were the stumps of some growth on each side of the forehead.

"Why wasn't this reported to the Police?"

The fat man raised his hand. "Now, now. In due time. We wanted to do a little investigating on our own, first. As you know, the CHA has worked hand in glove with the Police since its inception. We've only done what we thought right."

"And is this why I've been called here?"

"That's right."

"What for?"

"To enlist your aid, of course."

"What do you mean?"

"It's simple. This body was discovered last month in Nebraska. As you know, Bess Marshall disappeared after the lynching. Our operatives traced her to Nebraska. It was there she had this——" he grimaced—"child."

"So what?"

"So this. We sent our man to the county clerk who had so conveniently kept mum about the recorded marriage. Well, that wasn't all he kept mum about. No, sir.

We had to beat—use extreme measures to get the information from him, but by God, we got it, and *here it is!*"

So saying, the fat man lifted a thick volume from a desk drawer, its pages yellowed, its binding broken.

The Protector bent over to read the faded words on the cover. "Birth Records, 2045-2050 A.D., Federal City, Colorado."

THE BRAT followed the grasshoppers into a green-swarded valley, two miles from the farmhouse. A stream the width of a man's body flowed crookedly down the center of the valley, entering a natural tunnel in the face of a hillside. It was right into the tunnel they hopped, droves of them, right into the darkness. The brat ran after them, unconsciously leaping in imitation of the insects he pursued. But when they disappeared into the tunnel, the brat stopped.

He was frightened of the uncompromising darkness. The night was a darkness he could understand, a cloak of things familiar. But a tunnel . . . He sat down to consider the problem.

An ant crawled across his hand.

"Where are you going?" he asked.

"Busy, busy, busy," said the ant.

The brat flicked it from his thumb. Then he got to his feet and started for the tunnel.

It wasn't quite so dark when he entered. The stream still bubbled here, its sound echoing. He walked on further, looking for the grasshoppers.

Then he saw them faintly, gathering into a lawn-like thickness, surrounding something, somebody. It was a boy, about his age, only not really like him. Different, with an elongated head and pale skin, and long antennas waving out of his forehead.

"Hello," he said.

The boy looked up, startled. Then with a sudden spring, he threw himself on the brat, forcing him to the ground and pinioning his arms to his side.

PROTECTOR First Class Remington said to his superior:

"I remembered his name after I left. It used to be Lewis. Herman Lewis."

Chief Protector Harris answered: "So? And now it's Turesco?"

"Right. He was with some other organization a while back—maybe even a few of them. They were the race-haters. Professional rabble-rousers."

"Mm." Harris swung his feet off the desk. "No, Ward, I don't think so."

"Why not?"

"The CHA has been lending us a hand right down along the line. Sure, I know you don't like the idea of their own private police force—"

"Do you?"

"—but there are other things, too. They've got a string of charities that takes a big burden off the taxpayer's shoulder. They don't preach any hate doctrines. They get out of hand once in a while, but—"

"You mean like lynching."

The Chief said nothing.

"Like lynching the Geminite," continued Ward. "Like that."

Harris was silent. He picked up the glossy prints of the Geminite-Child and studied them. "What about this?" he asked finally.

"Turesco showed me a birth record book they took from the county clerk at the little town the Geminite lived in. It seems the Geminite and Bess Marshall have other offspring besides that poor dead thing there. Turesco wants to enlist our aid in finding them. He feels that they're a menace to society."

"Can't that omnipresent organization of his dig them up?"

"That's the point. They can't. They traced Bess Marshall to Nebraska, but that's as far as they got. They haven't the faintest idea where the kids are. And one thing's got them worried. Mendel."

"Mendel?"

"The CHA's afraid that one, maybe two of the Marshall kids take after their mother. They can spot one of those—" he gestured towards the photographs— "but they'd have a hell of a time recognizing the brat if he looked like *that*." The Protector pointed to the framed desk-photo of the Chief's own son.

"What are they afraid of?"

"Cross-breeding. The Geminite's already proved that the races are compatible. Now, they're afraid the kids'll grow up and marry and have other kids—maybe ordinary kids, maybe gray-faced kids with long heads and antennas. They want to nip this 'race problem' in the bud."

"And what are we supposed to do about it?"

"Find 'em. Put our scentists to work on it. The CHA's helpless. They specialize in thugs, goons, smart lawyers—"

The Chief interrupted. "Do they have any clues, anything we can start with?"

"Not much. Bess Marshall might have had her kids anytime during the past twenty-five years. Whether she sent them out on their own, took them with her, or what—they don't know. She kept to herself,

just like her husband. Turesho told me that his men questioned her, but couldn't get a sensible answer."

The Chief looked at him.

"She's mad," Ward said.

"I see." The Chief swiveled around and faced his desk. He drummed lightly on the glass top. Remington took off his helmet and examined the lining. His action was careless, but there was a tightness around his mouth. He said:

"Well? Do we play ball?"

"I don't know. I'll have to investigate the legal end first."

"Don't bother." Ward slammed his helmet back on his head, a sinking feeling in his chest. "That's sewed up. It's a charity project. They want to find those poor kids so they can take care of them. Yeah. On the operating table."

He stood up and walked out, his shoulders unnaturally high.

The Chief picked up his phone and called the Police laboratory.

THE BRAT looked down at the supine figure at his feet. He closed his eyes and tuned out the annoying sound of the grasshoppers, squeaking and chittering in anger.

His eyes had become accustomed to the darkness. He knelt down by the boy's side and examined his face. It was oddly familiar, yet it made him feel uneasy. The boy's face was gray, like the rocks bordering the stream.

His fingers reached out and touched the wire-like protuberance sprouting around his forehead. The body of the gray boy quivered. Quickly, the brat jerked his hand away and rose uncertainly to his feet.

The stream still flowed nearby, thinner now in the greenless ground beneath the tunnel, flowing towards some unguessable destination. The brat went over to it and filled his cupped hands. He brought it to the gray boy and dropped the water over his face. The two antennae suddenly stiffened, but the body remained still.

Then the gray boy opened his eyes.

"Hello," said the brat. "Are you all right?"

"Who are you?"

The brat thought this over. "Nobody. Who are you?"

The gray boy lifted himself by his elbows. "I am Ars Tenz Li," he said, his voice proud. A faraway look shone in his large eyes. He looked through and beyond the brat as he said: "Dead is my Home, so I take to my heart the Green Land; Dead is my Past, so I take to my bosom the Future."

"Who taught you that?" asked the brat. "Is it a poem? I know a poem. It's called Ozymandias."

"That's a funny name."

"No funnier'n yours. Can you talk to grasshoppers?"

The gray boy started. His large eyes narrowed as he drew himself up from the floor, suspicious, ready for anything.

"No, he said sullenly. "Of course not."

"Oh." The brat was disappointed. "I thought because—" His eyes lit up. "I can, a little. Watch." He reached down and picked up one of the green insects from the throng around them.

"Hello," he said.

"Hello," said the grasshopper.

"Did you hear him?" The brat turned to the gray boy, his eyes shining with delight. "Did you— What's the matter? What's wrong?"

The gray boy shrank back against the rock wall.

"Who are you?"

PROTECTOR Remington walked into the Police laboratory. He went straight to where Chief Harris was talking earnestly to the head physicist. He caught Harris' words:

".... radio. Shut off all radio communication in the area, and focus our beams. The slightest—oh, hello, Ward."

"Chief; Dr. Frankel."

"I think we've hit on it," said the Chief. "Frankel's sure the antenna will react to a strong raido beam, and vice-versa. There's an insect strain in these Geminites."

"So? Going to broadcast to them? 'Baby won't you please come home'!"

Dr. Frankel, eyebrows raised, said: "I'm afraid I—"

"Don't mind him, Doctor," Hariss said. "Remington doesn't quite take to the idea."

"Oh? Why not?"

"Listen, Chief." Remington licked his lips. "Why does this have to be a CHA project? Why don't we handle it our own way, without calling in that gang? Can't we take care of our own—foundlings."

The doctor snorted. "Foundlings? You mean hybrids!"

"I mean foundlings! You know why CHA wants those kids. Why can't our own welfare agencies take on the job? Why do we have to kow-tow to them, just because they found out about Bess Marshall's kids? Now that we know, we can proceed on our own."

Harris flushed. "I'm afraid you don't understand. The CHA's a recognized charity organization. We're just lending a hand. It's a private matter."

Ward looked defeated. "What's the first step?"

"Radio," said Frankel. "We're issuing directives to all Nebraska stations and ham operators to

cease operations at a specified hour tomorrow afternoon. Then we'll send out our strongest radio beams — an excellent chance to experiment with the new Kohler Wavex, by the way — and pick up any signals we can get. There'll probably be a lot of false alarms, but well have enough men on hand to investigate them all. We'll find them if they're in the state. At least, that's my theory."

"I see. Who's going?"

The Chief answered: "Ten groups will stand by. I'll be in charge of one of them. Then there'll be the group that Turesco will be with." He paused. "You'll be in charge of that. Of course, there's every likelihood that we won't find any other Geminite. They could have wandered all over creation by this time. But anyway — we'll try it. What can we lose?"

"I don't know," said Remington dully.

THE gray boy took the brat by the hand and led him into the dark recesses of the tunnel. He cautioned him about each loose rock and pitfall, guided him sure-footedly on a path he seemed to know very well.

It was at the Stygian point of their journey, when the brat's heart thumped wildly in his chest in fear of the darkness, that the gray boy released the brat's hand and left him standing there, quaking, helpless in the enveloping nothingness. Then suddenly, there was a burst of light. The sides of the tunnel reflected the light from a cave, cut directly into the wall. The cave was brilliantly lighted, a light which emanated from two thin pencils of glass, perched on ledges on each side of the walls.

"It was my father's," said the gray boy, pointing a long finger at the radiant sticks. "He gave them to me when—"

"When what?" asked the brat.

"I don't remember."

"Was it your father who taught you the poem?"

"Yes."

The gray boy walked to the corner of the cave and dropped to his knees. From a pile of miscellaneous objects, he took a mesh bag and began fingering the cord. The brat watched him carefully, trying to guess what the round-shaped things inside the bag were.

His host lifted one out. "Oranges," he said.

The brat leaped for the fruit. He was very hungry.

PROTECTOR Remington was sorry now that he had let Turesco talk him into using the CHA's Copter instead of the usual Police craft. And he was unhappy about the two officers assigned to the group. They seemed all right, outwardly — young, and cleancut. But Ward imagined he saw something cruel in the cast of their eyes and the set of their jaws.

One of the officers was busy with the small, compact Wavex, checking its Morse-like signals with the chart in his hand. The other had earphones on his head and was talking in low tones to the Police broadcasting unit, where the beams were emanating.

Suddenly, he whipped off the phones and turned — not to the Protector, but to Turesco.

"They got 'em," he said.

Turesco said nothing, but Ward heard his sharp intake of breath.

"They heard one word," continued the officer.

"What was it?"

"*Good!*"

Turesco grinned. "Get your instructions. Then get to wherever it is. But fast. I want to be there first."

THE brat examined the U-shaped tubing curiously.

"And your father gave you this?" he said in wonder. The word "father" had taken on new meaning for the brat.

"Yes. It works when you squeeze it," said the gray boy. "Only don't squeeze it at anybody. It hurts."

Fascinated, the brat pointed the two open ends of the tubing at the rock wall and squeezed the curved end. The thing shot out a beam of blue-gray light. Where the beam struck the wall, there arose a faint mist of pulverized rock. When it cleared, there was a slight depression in the wall.

"That's how I made the cave," the other explained. "It was just a tunnel when I got here, so I made a cave with this."

"Gee." The brat was awe-struck. He aimed the tubing at the wall again, and was just about to press the end, when the headache that had caused him so much past misery struck him suddenly. The pain was terrible. He put the tubing on the ground and held the heel of his palm against his forehead. He would have cried out, had the other not been there to hear.

But the gray boy wouldn't have heard a thing. As if by some mysterious signal, he had fallen against the wall, burying his long head in his arms. The brat heard the thud as his body hit the ground, and trying to forget his own pain, he hurried over to him.

Then the pain became more intense. He had had such headaches before — chiefly in the cities — but now it was almost unbearable. He fell to his knees and began to sob aloud. He dug his face into the gritty sand and rock of the cave floor and strained his small fists against the ground. Then he cried out.

PROTECTOR Remington had meant to be the first to enter the tunnel, but somehow the other officers had managed to get between him and the entrance, and it was Turesco who went in first.

Ward shut off the portable Wavex and put it carefully on the grass, a few feet from the small stream which bubbled on into the mouth of the tunnel. Then he started after the fat man, his pocket Light Tube in his hand.

"Over here!" came Turesco's voice, now a booming harshness. Ward hurried in the direction of the sound. He saw the light.

"Look!" Turesco was gleeful. "They've got a cave lit up with two glass sticks. Some of that Geminite-science. Look at 'em!"

Ward put his Light back in his hip pocket and knelt down beside the two prone figures on the floor of the cave. One was gray-skinned, with an elongated head and now limp antennas growing out of his forehead. The other was a boy; just a boy.

"Are they both—"

"Of course they are!" cried the fat man. "Both of 'em, the Geminite's sons. See — the Wavex put 'em out of commission." The smile left his face. "Go outside," he said to one of the officers. "Don't let anybody in till we get out." He turned to Ward as the officer left. "Bring them around," he demanded.

Ward was doing that already. He chafed their wrists, wet their lips with stream water. It took ten minutes. The boy came around first.

"What is it?" he said.

"Easy son." The Protector cradled the young head in his elbow. "You'll be all right."

"Ozymandias —"

"Who?"

"No—" the boy shook his head, as if to clear it. "Not Ozymandias. Ars —"

"What's he saying?" The fat man had started to perspire. "Lemme talk to him." He put his big hand on the boy's shoulder. "Listen, kid," he said. "Listen to me. Do you remember your father?"

The boy stared at him, uncomprehendingly.

"Leave him, Turesco," Ward said.

"Your father, remember?"

"Turesco —"

"Shut up!" the fat man shouted. "I'm handling this!"

The Protector's lips tightened.

"Where'd you get that idea? I'm in charge here."

Turesco smirked, and squeezed the boy's shoulder harder. "Listen, brat! I'm talking to you! Tell us about your father!"

"*Turesco!*" The blood rushed to Ward's head.

"Shut *up*, damn it!" The perspiration was like a coating of oil over the fat man's face now, and behind the film, his skin was feverish and red, the eyes hot.

"I'm warning you!" said the Protector tensely, his control leaving him. "Let the boy alone."

Turesco looked up, hate twisting his features — not hate for a man, for Remington, for the boy beneath his hand; it was sheer hate in the abstract; ugly, terrifying.

With a snarl, the fat man struck the boy across the mouth.

THINGS happened fast. Ward, in blind anger, made a rush for Turesco, but as he did, the remaining officer lunged to break the Protector's charge. There was a scramble. Suddenly, the officer stiffened, screamed, then fell, clutching the small of his back with his hand.

Remington whirled. The gray-skinned boy had propped himself up on his elbows. In his hand was a U-shaped tubing, faintly glowing with a blue-gray light.

"See?" Turesco's scream was almost hysterical. "Murderers! Killers! He killed him!" He stared wildly at the gray boy, his finger pointing accusingly.

"It's all right now, son," said Ward, trying to keep his voice steady. "Put it down."

The boy's eyes were pleading. He put down the weapon.

"Blucher!" the fat man was screaming. "Blucher!"

The officer who had been posted outside came running into the cave.

"Your own guards, Turesco? I should have known."

"Blucher!"

"What's wrong?" Blucher had his pistol drawn.

"He killed Marley!" cried the fat man. "*Shoot him!*"

Ward was stunned.

"NO!" he shouted. It was too late. The officer stood at the entrance, feet braced against the recoil, and pumped bullet after bullet into the figure on the floor, and left it writhing and twisting, clutching at its wounds in the last agonies of death.

Suddenly, Turesco was very calm.

"Now take the boy," he said softly, "and we'll go to the Copter."

All the Protector's control had left him. "You won't get away with it Turesco!" he shouted,

shaking with his rage. "It's murder! I'll get you for it!"

The fat man smiled. "How would you do that? It would be just as easy to have Blucher kill you, too, you know. Then we'd say it was the boy who did it. As it is, I'd rather the authorities found only one dead man in the cave — two, if you want to count *that*." His face softened. "Listen, Remington — this is all very unfortunate, but if you only knew —"

"Knew what?"

"That this was all for the best. It is, you know."

Blucher lifted the boy gently and walked out with him. Turesco's hand reached out and fell on the Protector's shoulder. He winked.

"Relax," he said.

Then he turned and went out.

* * *

Remington walked slowly across the field, through the tall grass, his helmet dangling by the strap from his hand.

He watched the copter rise serenely into the air and then level off into horizontal flight. When it was out of sight, he dropped to the soft ground and opened the top button of his tunic. He had a headache.

An ant crawled slowly across the back of his hand. He lifted it to eye level.

"Hello," he said.

"Busy, busy, busy," said the ant.

Speed Limit!

★ ★

CONSIDERING only the development of jet planes and rocket ships for use in the atmosphere —that's all we have today—what limitations on them can we expect? Are speeds limited, for example?

The answer is 'yes'—the handwriting on the wall can be seen. From a power standpoint, it would appear that rockets and jets for use in the atomsphere can be built to attain almost any speed — already they've hit close to 2000 miles per hour. Such speeds are simply terrific considering that the ships are powering through air — and that of course is the limiting factor. Air resistance causes skin friction and its consequent heating. The result is that the ship gets hot enough to melt its skin! For a jet to go high enough for thin air means that its engines won't operate. That doesn't bother a rocket —but when it goes high enough, it's a space ship!

It seems that scientists visualize jet airliners with a top speed of about a thousand miles per hour. This will be more than fast enough for ordinary passenger transport. Anything over that, can be left to the rockets, which are not atmospheric craft anyway. That thousand mile-per-hour figure comes from a balancing of fuel consumption, speed, weight and skin friction. Metallurgy is supplying heat-resistant titanium metal for jet planes. The engines are already here. Thousand mile an hour speeds are coming—and fast . . . for air transport fifteen hundred mile an hour speeds are a bit too high . . .

G. LEEWAY

"For a man who failed he looks very happy!"

Buck just wanted to hunt squirrels that
day when the little green and red fellers came
a'feuding. Well, sir, the goin's on we called —

Buck and the Space War

by

Mack Reynolds

THERE'S some folks in this here world just naturally has things happen. There's some can go through life every day just practically like the one before but there's some like Buck Willard that just practically everything happens to.

Now take Buck. Some ordinary sapsucker might go out onto the St. John's river to try and get hisself a bass or maybe a mess of specks and if he didn't catch nothing it'd just purely be because they wasn't biting or maybe he was using the wrong bait, maybe a plug instead of shiners or maybe worms instead of sulphur minnows. Anyway this ordinary feller wouldn't catch no fish for ordinary reasons. But not Buck.

If Buck goes out to catch hisself a bass and he don't come back with one it's sure to be some reason'd bowl most folks over in their shoes like the time he seen the sea serpent come up the St. John's maybe to spawn or something.

So many things happen to Buck that some folks around Dupont— Dupont is on the St. John's maybe ninety-five, hundred miles south of Jacksonville — don't believe more'n half what he tells. They ain't got no proof against him, nobody never caught Buck Willard in no lie yet, but even his nearest kin will admit some of the things that happen to Buck is way out of the accustomed.

Some times what happens to Buck is so *far* out of accustomed it's all a man can do to pry it out of him. You can set around all evening at Nan's juke a trying to pry out of Buck what happened to him and it's all you can do. Buck's kind of modest, suppose you'd say.

Particular thing brought this to mind was the time Buck went

out to shoot hisself a mess of squirrels not too far away, maybe two, three miles from where Randy Sauls has his cat fish camp near to the mouth of Lake Dexter. Was along in November which is slow for guiding seeing the tourists don't come down for the bass mostly until along in January and Buck was tired setting around the juke just jawing with Otis Martin and the other guides which ain't got nothing to do with themselves.

So this morning early Buck decides to go out and get hisself a mess of squirrels, maybe knock off a few coot on the way home. Some people don't think much of coot but if you let them set over night in vinegar it takes a lot of that coot taste out. Otis Martin and Nan kind of kid Buck a mite about his hunting and how they'd be surprised if he come back with more than one, two squirrels at most but he's real quiet and ain't really bragging atall when he tells them he figures he's probably the best squirrel hunter this side of Kentucky.

Anyway Buck goes on down to the municipal dock and gets into his boat. He wraps the kicker rope around the wheel, hits the choke button a couple of licks with the heel of his hand, yanks the rope and is off, shoving his way on through the hyacinth beds out to the open stream.

Now if Buck had just in mind getting hisself three, four squirrels he could of stopped off near Jules Hawkins' shiner camp and knocked off that many but he was a mite nettled from what Otis and Nan had been asaying about his hunting so he figured he'd get himself a mess and a mess for Nan and one for Otis too and end once and for all the talk about his ability to get squirrels.

So he kicked on up past the bait camp and up onto the flats near beacon fifteen and then he cut down, like I say, past Randy Saul's little camp. Finally he finds the place he wants, all away from everything, maybe fifteen, twenty miles from the nearest road folks could come in by. There's some think Florida is all like Miami or maybe Tampa or Daytona Beach, don't realize there's some of the purely wildest country ever right into the middle of it.

Buck beached his boat there and takes up his single barrel twelve gauge and a couple hands full of number six shells and walks rea. quiet into the woods.

YOU know the way squirrel hunting is. You find yourself maybe a old stump or a log and you sit on it and keep still as can be. The woods around Dupont are mostly like jungle with cypress, live oak with lots of Spanish moss and lots of palms. Bye and bye any squirrels might have heard you come up forget about it and start going about squirrel business and crashing from one palm tree to another and barking and that's the way you locate the little sap-suckers.

That's the way it is usual, but not today. Buck's there not more'n maybe five minutes when he sees a glint like the sun reflecting on something way up above, thinks maybe its one of the passenger airplanes coming down from the north with a load of tourists heading for Miami. But it ain't. The glint gets brighter and brighter and Buck looks up and *Whoosssh* there's a rush of air like and a blinding light like and *Whoosssh* something comes a sweeping down and lands into a little clearing can't be more than ten, fifteen feet from where Buck is sitting real quiet waiting for the squirrels to make a noise.

Buck says later he recalls the

thing as being kind of round like a saucer but it moves so fast almost like a blur he can't rightly remember too well.

No sooner has it come to rest here into this clearing than a door like, kind of round Buck says it was, not like a door you'd have onto a house, opens up and out comes, fast as he can move, a little feller'd go maybe three and a half, four feet high and green faced like a lime. He rolls hisself tail over elbow away from the saucer ship like and out of the clearing and into a kind of depression already half filled with swamp water. Winds up not mor'n a few yards from Buck.

Just in time too cause Buck sees another glint from up above and there's another *Whoosssh* and a bright light comes down, you'd think it was the beam from a big flashlight if'n it was night time but this was bright right in the midst of day. The light kind of touches the saucer ship and it starts smoking and melting away and before you could tell it was gone without one sign of where it'd been.

Course all this time Buck was a kind of sitting there gopping at these goings on. Here he was just waiting for a squirrel to start barking or maybe running from one tree to another. But, like I say, Buck is one of these folks things is always happening to so he

just figures it's a off day for squirrels and just goes on a setting there.

No sooner was this here first saucer ship all melted away and gone than *Whoosssh* down comes a second one almost like to the first only different a slight. Comes down and lands into the same clearing Buck is on the edge of and the little green feller in the ditch nearby, and another queer looking little feller about the same size as the first one but maybe almost twice as fat comes out. Buck says this one looks something like a tourist from Indianapolis only his face is colored like a red breasted bream.

Now Buck figures right off these two are from some other planet or something cause he can see they look more like some characters onto Bill Lungrun's TV set than anything else. Bill's got the only TV set in Dupont. Fact is, they look more like somebody from space than any into those shows like Space Cadet so Buck figures that must be what they are.

No sooner is the second one out of his space boat and kind of peering around, satisfied like with hisself, than this little green one was hiding in the hole near Buck ups with a funny looking gadget looks something like a section of rubber hose and squirts a beam at this second one.

Down goes the red faced one, just in time, and he rolls hisself out of the way and into a bed of a little stream, lucky for him its been a kind of dry fall and there ain't no water in it.

Well sir, it must've been a shock to the red one to find out the green one was still up and around and ready to continue the feud whatever its cause might've been. But he tugs a gadget of his own looked something like a eggbeater to Buck but never did get a very good look at it, and fires away with a kind of boiling violet light just misses the green one by inches and knocks half a dozen palm fronds offn a tree, cut off clean as a whistle.

BUCK sees the kind of beams and rays these fellers is cutting off at each other with and figures that if they don't look out they'll set a woods fire'd be a mercy to ever get out again it being so far and all away from a good road the rangers'd have one time ever getting to it. Besides, Buck is just about betwixt the two of them and he don't know how long it might be before one or t'other of them misses and hits him.

Now up to this here time neither of the two critters had spotted Buck they was too wrapped up in each other and too excited and here Buck was not more than a few yards away from the little green one.

Before he had time to think it out just what he was doing, he takes three, four strides and reaches out and picks up this here green one and swoops him up under his arm didn't weigh more than twenty-five, thirty pounds and starts for the second one shaking his old twelve gauge single barrel and hollering that if they didn't cut out all this talleyhootin around he'd give 'em what for.

Well, sir, you can imagine how surprised the two of them was. Here the green one finds hisself ketched up under Buck's arm and the red one he sees Buck a coming at him, all of a sudden, hadn't even seen him before Buck was sitting so quiet, a waving his twelve gauge and with the green one under his arm.

Before the red one could've upped with his eggbeater gadget Buck was to him and standing right in front of him maddern a hornet and yelling for him to cut out all this here folderol before they set fire to the woods.

The red one just stands there kind of blinking and a looking at the green one's tucked under Buck's arm and kicking and yelling in a shrill little voice like he was fit to be tied.

So Buck puts down the little feller onto the ground and kind of brushes him off a mite has a nice little uniform on but betwixt the water in that hole and all the dirt and leaves and everything he sure looked a mess now.

Both of them is speechless at the way this is turned out, they not expecting it, but Buck says, kind of mild now, "What're you two up to anyways? Got no more sense than to go chompin and howlin' around like this you'd think it was Saturday night at the juke."

The red one kind of glares at Buck and says, "If it hadn't been for your interference, this enemy of the chosen would have gone to join his misbegotten ancestors!"

The other one says something that sounds like, "Hah!" and his hand starts coming up again with his gadget but Buck frowns at him real hard so he puts it back into his belt.

Buck says, "All right now, supposing we just set down here and now and figure this out can't have you settin fire to the woods and cutting the trees down and all."

Well, they're still kind of dazed by Buck popping up all of a suden and getting them into a spot where they can't rightly use their gadgets on each other, so they kind of simmer down at least to the point where they just glare at each other whilst they answer Buck's questions.

Buck says, "First of all, how come you talk American, ain't hard to see you're from elsewheres?"

"Radio emanations," snaps the green one not taking his eyes from the red feller. "We the chosen race of Venus find it necessary at times to communicate with the Martian vermin. Rather than speak their degenerate tongue, or allow them to speak our lordly language, we compromised and use the language of Earth."

"I'll be dog," Buck said.

The red one gets mad as a hoot owl at that. "The opposite is true," he snaps out. "We Martians would not descend to speak the foul language of Venus nor have them learn our sacred tongue. Hence, *we* have compromised and learned your Earth language."

"Comes to the same thing," Buck murmurs, "seems as if. Let's git to the point, just what're you two doing all this here now scrapping about? Here you come hundreds of miles, maybe more, from your own places and what'd you do? Stead of going fishing together, Dupont's got the best bass fishing anywheres, you start banging away like a couple of crazy coot".

First they looked at him like

maybe he'd lost his propeller, didn't make no sense atall. The green one, kind of dignified like, says, "Venusians and Martians have been engaged in internecine warfare for millennia. While you comparatively backward Earthlings were still building pyramids on the Nile river, our every effort was already directed against each other."

Buck could see, right then and there, this was one awful feud going on twixt these green folks and red folks. He hadn't never heard of no Nile river couldn't have been very good bass water or he would've but that wasn't important anyways.

Buck says, "Let's talk this out a mite. Just what are you a warring for? With all them there gadgets and beams and all you must cut up each other something awful."

WELL, with that they both start accusin' each other of starting the big trouble but it comes out in no time atall that it all happened so far back neither rightly knows just what did happen.

So Buck says to them kind of gentle like since he didn't want them rarin' off again burning up the woods all the way from Silver Springs to Sanford, "Seems to me you all'd be better off if'n you tried being more neighborly."

That started them off again and Buck noticed they'd lost any antagonism like they mighta had against him and was just hollering twixt themselves. So he says, "Ain't you ever figured you oughta do to the other feller the way you'd like him to do you?"

Well, sir, you'd never believe it but that kind of stopped them and Buck could see both of them was thinking it out.

The red one kind of looks at him and says, "Earthling that is a beautiful thought." You can see he's set back.

The green one nods to that and is kind of frowning like. He kind of mumbles, "If everyone followed such a philosophy . . ." But then he shakes his head and scowls at the red one. "Possibly the chosen of Venus are capable of assimilating such a lofty ethic but we must defend ourselves against the vermin of Mars."

That started the little red feller off again but Buck hushed them both.

He said, "If folks haven't been getting along, it's the one *starts* being nice to t'other that's going to feel best about patching it up." He settles hisself down on the stump and says. "Now supposin one of you come up to me and whomped me one on the face. Supposin stead of whomping you back I just naturally turned my face about so as to give you another chance? Now how'd you feel about that?"

Well, that set them back again. You could see them little fellers no matter what size or color they might be, was ready thinkers.

Buck says, "Now here's the same idea only put a different way." He notices that the little red one has took out a little pad like and is noting down in a funny scribbling writing what Buck says. "It's purely better to give somebody else something nice than it is to get something given yourself. It makes you feel better like inside "

Well, sir, you'd never believe how quick those two took to what Buck was a telling them. No time atall there they was sitting side by side listening to him. And pretty soon the red one is apologizing to the green one for burning up his saucer ship, and the green one says not to make nothing of it cause it was getting old and rusty anyways and it was practically a favor what with it being insured and all.

Bucks says, "If you all listen into our radio, how come you ain't already heard these ideas? Most every morning, specially Sundays, you can tune in on these here ideas."

But the green one says, "Holy One, we of the other planets had no idea your teachings could be heard on radio. The few times we attempted to tune in upon morning broadcasts we . . ." he kind of shuddered here " . . . were unfortunate to receive, ah *soap operas,* I believe they are called. To avoid them we have listened only to programs from noon on, most of them news broadcasts. And I assure you, Holy One, there is nothing in them to suggest that your fellow Earthlings have ever heard of your teachings."

Finally Buck figures he hasn't got all day to waste away jawing so he stand up and says, "Well, I have to be getting along. You two fellers oughta go on back where you come from and tell your folks what I said. Ain't no sense in feuding away like you do. Never get nothing worthwhile accomplished."

BY this time they was both kind of hanging their heads and the both of them'd been taking down notes, each in his own hand writing, and every time they look up at Buck their eyes kind of shine like.

So the red one says, "Holy One, do you mean that you commission us to return to our respective planets and spread your word?"

Buck thinks about that and says, "Why sure. More folks get to hearing the way they should act, better it'll be."

"We hear and we obey," says the green one and the red one he says that all the people on Mars is ready to hear such ideas and they'll spread over the planet like a brush fire and the green one he allows Venus is the same way.

So the two of them, kind of bowing their heads, back away from Buck to the one remaining saucer ship and they climb into it, friendly to each other as can be, and off they go *Whoossh*.

Buck kinds of looks after them for a minute and says out loud, "Shucks, I wonder if them little fellers got the idea all them teachings was mine original."

When he sees how late it is, Buck is kind of vexed on account of he didn't have a squirrel to his name. But he figures it couldn't be helped so he just naturally goes on back to his boat, starts her up and kicks on back to Dupont.

When he saunters back into Nan's juke, there Otis Martin still is having a can of beer and setting on a stool jawing with Nan. They both see he don't have no squirrels but they don't say nothing to Buck, just kind of grin.

Buck takes a stool hisself but he don't order no beer. He just sits there for a time and thinks.

Finally he says to nobody in particular, "Sometimes I wonder if'n we got any right to go off into the woods and shoot them little squirrels. Maybe they got just as much right to live as us."

Well, that sets Nan and Otis off to laughing, they not really understanding at that time what's behind Buck's word and not knowing the real reason he come back without a mess of squirrels. They just purely figure Buck is trying to find some excuse for his bad luck.

Otis laughs loudest, him and Buck being rivals in the tourist guide business and him liking to get a chance to make Buck look poorly. He laughs and says to Nan, "Buck Willard the natural born evangelist. Can you imagine Buck being a evangelist?"

"Oh, I don't know," says Buck.

129

Printed in Great Britain
by Amazon